Blood and Time

Amaranthine Vampires Trilogy
Book 1

TP Donohue

ISBN: 978-0-6459147-1-9 (eBook)

ISBN: 978-0-6459147-0-2 (paperback)

Editor: Lacey Braziel

Cover design: Victoria Cooper Design

Interior design and formatting: Cassie Weaver

Published in Australia by Wordfare Publishing

Words move, music moves
Only in time;
but that which is only living
Can only die
- T.S. Eliot., 'Burnt Norton,' The Four Quartets

Chapter 1

David

Detective Sergeant David Sorrow knew it was a bloodless crime scene before he set foot in the tiny flat. He had a keen sense for blood, like all his kind. But blood wasn't an addiction for him. Not like it was for the Bloodborn vampires. He needed it to survive, just as humans needed water, but he wasn't controlled by it.

The victim's flat was on the second floor of a run-down apartment complex with a forgettable exterior. Inside, it was minimally furnished. A light-coloured sofa, a wooden coffee table and a small dining set. Everything looked to be in its place. No signs of violence or forced entry. Nevertheless, a woman's lifeless body lay on the kitchen floor.

Slipping on a pair of latex gloves, he squatted beside her. She had a pale, freckled face with a thin nose, framed by curly red hair. She was young, maybe mid or late twenties, clothed in jeans and a button-down shirt. All humans had their own unique scent, and though the pall of death now hung over her, the woman still had a muted perfume that reminded him of dried roses. He gently turned her head. Purplish bruising had bloomed across her eye socket and brow bone, the blood pooling under the skin, radiating from the lump on the back of her head.

Claire Morton, one of the detectives on his team, had taken charge of processing the scene. 'Her name is Anna Steenberger. We think time of death was late last night, or in the early hours of this morning. We're treating it as a probable homicide. Looks like blunt force trauma to the back of the head – either she was hit from behind with something or fell against something with force. The post-mortem will tell us more of course.' She spoke over David's shoulder.

David liked working with Morton. She was thorough, efficient, and smart. He had overheard her talking with Craig Orbost, one of the forensic analysts, as he was arriving. Their conversation had caused him to pause for a moment in the stairwell outside the flat.

'Who caught this case?' Orbost had asked.

'Sorrow,' Morton replied.

Orbost whistled through his teeth. 'Paul Rudd, you mean?'

'What?'

'Well, he's like Paul Rudd, isn't he? He's been in the job what – ten, fifteen years? But he never seems to get any older. I wish I knew what he was doing. Creams? Surgery? Botox?'

'No idea,' Morton said gruffly. She was rarely drawn

into gossip about her colleagues. Another reason David liked her.

But the conversation bothered him. It wasn't that he minded the nickname. Australians loved nicknames. It was how they showed affection. But in another few years, his age-defying looks would start to become problematic. Again.

I need to talk to Rafael about that.

He rose to his feet beside the woman's body and Morton took half a step backwards, flicking a page over on the small notepad in her hand.

'Who found her?' David asked.

Morton glanced at her notepad. 'The neighbour, Mrs Swan, phoned it in around 7:00 a.m. She locked herself out after her morning walk and Anna kept her spare key. She came over and found the door unlocked.'

David nodded, shifting his weight as he glanced around the flat.

'Any relatives? A flat mate? Partner?' Morton shook her head.

'Not that we are aware of at this stage. We door-knocked the other neighbours. She lived alone, and none of them saw or heard anything out of place last night.' She showed David a transparent evidence bag that held a photo ID. 'This might help, though. She was a student at the Sigma Institute.'

David took the bag and held it up to the light. As he was examining the ID, a sharp, slightly woody odour caught his attention, unmistakable to his heightened senses. It wasn't a vampire scent. He was sure of that.

But it wasn't the victim's scent, either. It was the lingering essence of another human presence, whispering secrets from the night before. He handed the evidence bag back to Morton absently and edged his way towards the smell, following the direction where it seemed to get stronger.

'Sorrow?' Morton queried, trailing behind him. David stopped in his tracks. He heard Rafael's words in his ears as clearly as if he were in the room with him.

There are only two rules that must never be broken. Protect humanity from the Bloodborns. Protect the Amaranthines' secret.

'Good work here, Morton,' David said, turning back to her. 'I know I don't need to tell you this, but let's make sure we get official statements from all the neighbours. Hopefully someone saw something. Talk to Mrs Swan again and nail down the timeline. Hopefully forensics will turn up something in the way of fingerprints or other evidence.'

'Yes, sir, the forensics are almost finished,' Morton said. 'I've also asked the analysts to start working the other angles – bank accounts, search history, socials.'

'Excellent,' David said. 'I'll reach out to the Institute and speak to anyone who might have known her there. We may be able to track down next of kin that way.'

'You also need to see this,' Morton beckoned him. David raised his chin slightly. It couldn't be a second body. No one had mentioned it when he was called in and his keen sense of smell told him only one truly dead person was on the premises.

Morton led him through the kitchen and down a hall to the bedroom.

'Can we come in?' she asked from the doorway.

'Sure, I've just about finished here,' Orbost said.

As they entered the room, Morton gestured to the wall opposite the messily made-up double bed. It was covered from ceiling to floor with black paint and there was a strange array of chalk symbols scribbled across it. The chalk was smudged in places, as if the writer had hastily erased some symbols and replaced them.

'Any idea what these are?' David asked, moving towards the wall. He ran his gloved finger lightly along the chalk and turned to look at Morton.

'No. It might be connected to her work at the Institute,' offered Morton. 'There's also this,' she said, stepping around Orbost to pull open a cupboard door. David noticed the usual items hanging inside: clothing, a few handbags and belts. But the back of the door was covered with photos, various clippings and some pencil sketches. There were snippets of articles and printouts of long lines of computer coding. One photo was of a woman, her blonde hair pulled back and an unsmiling face staring straight at the camera. She was wearing academic regalia, including a puffy black hat with a red ribbon and holding a ceremonial staff in her left hand. The photo was marked with graffiti. Someone had used permanent marker to give the woman a set of horns and morph the staff into a pitchfork. David stared at the woman's face for a moment and felt a brief stirring of recognition pass over him. As he grasped for the memory, it slipped out of reach. Being around for over a century made it hard to keep track of all the memories, all the people. Had he seen her face somewhere before? Maybe. Maybe not.

'It's kind of odd, isn't it?' Morton said, frowning.

David took out his phone and moved about, snapping photos of the wall and the door.

'Very odd, indeed,' he agreed. 'The blonde woman in the photo – do we know who she is?'

Morton shook her head.

'It certainly seems she was known to our victim,' David said, pointing at the pitchfork. Orbost laughed and David saw a rare grin cross Morton's face.

'Based on her academic gown and hat, she might be linked to the Institute too. Maybe they can help identify her?'

'Good thinking,' Morton said, scribbling in her notebook.

'I'll head over to the Institute now to see if I can speak with anyone who knew her. Maybe they can shed light on the symbols too. Call me when the post-mortem is done, Morton?' David asked over his shoulder as he headed back to the kitchen.

'Of course,' Morton confirmed, flipping the notebook closed.

Moving past Anna's body, David caught the spruce scent again. It was definitely from a recent visitor. Since Anna lived alone, it stood to reason that the scent may belong to whoever was with her when she died. There was no damage to the front door, and no sign of a struggle, which meant whoever it was, she had probably invited them in. But he would have to wait and see if the forensics report turned up any tangible evidence. Human scents were as unique to him as fingerprints, but unlike fingerprints, there was no database for scents.

Stepping out onto the brightly lit street below, David shielded his eyes from the morning glare. He unlocked the police car and slid in behind the wheel. Taking out his pocket watch, he flicked it open to check the time, then closed it again. He knew he didn't need it anymore. He could tell the time on his phone or the car stereo, but the solid weight of it in his palm always helped him to focus. He sat holding it for a moment, absorbing the stir of anticipation he always felt at the beginning of an investigation. Leaning forwards, he keyed in the Institute's name to the car's navigation system. It would be a good half hour drive to get there. Slipping the watch back into his breast pocket, he reversed the car out onto the road, threading his way through the morning traffic.

Chapter 2

Essie

Essie jumped when her research assistant slammed the door to her office hard enough to rattle the walls. Ben Chu was the nephew of the Institute's provost, Angela Chu, who was also Essie's boss. Angela said he had research experience and would be an asset, but since he had arrived at the Institute, he had been far more interested in staring at his phone than doing any research. He had also managed to spill hot tea all over Essie's laptop, feed a pile of last year's exam papers through a shredder and accidentally copied an email to his girlfriend to the entire faculty. That was just in his first week.

Still, beggars couldn't be choosers, and when it came to research assistants, Essie had little luck. In the past two years, she had been through four assistants, each one worse than the last. And if she wanted to win the faculty promotion that was up for grabs this year, she would need the help, any help. Plus, he was Angela's nephew. So, instead of yelling at Ben for slamming the door, she grimaced and turned her eyes back to her computer. Pushing a strand of her hair out of her face, she tucked it behind her ear and squinted at the screen.

There were fifty or so unread emails, and she had twenty minutes before she had to give her first lecture of the semester to the first year class, in a hall across campus. Most of the emails were the usual invitations to write for journals or speak at upcoming conferences. It was satisfying being known as the preeminent academic in the field of temporal physics, but all the peripheral stuff that went with it was mostly a bore. When she started at the Institute, *Vogue* magazine had contacted her to do a profile piece on her for a 'Women in Science' feature. If pressed, she would admit that she had found it tempting. It felt like she had won a popularity contest. She had spent most of her life locked out of popularity contests because the rules were all a mystery to her. But then logic had prevailed, and she saw the flattery for what it really was – a distracting waste of time. Not to mention it presented certain risks. Raising her profile might attract attention. A cold shiver snaked down her spine as the sound of a woman's voice, like a small bell, echoed through her head. Her eyes flickered from her laptop to the black backpack on her desk. She patted the bag, visualising the little green notebook tucked away inside, safe and sound.

Turning back to her laptop screen, Essie quickly deleted all the speaking invitations and replied to an email from her friend Cecil, a retired colleague, asking to reschedule dinner with her. He was feeling unwell. She made a mental note to check on him later. She was about to bin the rest of the emails when one subject line made her muscles tense: *Gilbert Thornton – Update*. Her hand hovered over the mouse. After a moment, she drew a breath and braced herself as she opened it and scanned the contents.

As of this date, we have no further leads on your father's disappearance. This case will be assigned to a new officer, and we will get back in touch.

She sighed out the breath she had been holding while she was reading. The police, it seemed, were giving up on finding her missing father. Almost two years had passed since he disappeared. Gilbert Thornton had owned his own Italian restaurant. Essie had practically grown up in the restaurant kitchen. Then, he went to a hospitality conference in Melbourne one week and never returned. All the leads seemed to have gone nowhere and now the police were assigning a new case officer. She had a strong suspicion that 'assigning a new case officer' was the phrase the Missing Persons Unit used when the current officer had run out of ideas, and they were shuffling the problem off to someone else. She clutched the fabric of her shirt, her heart heavy. The grief of missing him, of not knowing what had happened, was one thing. But what gnawed at her most was the guilt she felt for her part in it, for not giving the police all the information she had.

The door banged open, and Essie jumped again, her temper flaring. Slamming the laptop closed, she readied herself to give Ben a piece of her mind.

'Essie! What the hell do you think you're doing?' A broad woman in an ill-fitting maroon skirt burst into her office. Ben was two steps behind her, and as Essie glanced over the woman's shoulder, he made a worried face before shrugging and backing away slowly.

'Good morning, Professor,' Essie said, trying to keep her voice calm.

'Don't "professor" me, Essie. How could you speak to a student that way? And in front of a gathering of new recruits! Someone was recording it on their phone and now the clip has gone viral!'

Angela Chu held up her phone and stuck it in Essie's face. It was already replaying footage from the Internship Induction workshop the Institute had run the day before. Essie watched for a moment with a growing sense of unease. She recalled her PhD student asking her a question about the Zion's Loop equation in front of the new interns.

'So, the Zion's Loop cannot be solved?' Anna Steenberger asked. The camera darted from Anna back to Essie's face. A million thoughts had raced through her head as she had tried to think of a suitable answer at the time. Telling the truth was out of the question, of course. She saw reflected in her own eyes the exact moment when she had decided the best option would be to go on the offensive.

Snorting unattractively in response to Steenberger's question, she snapped, 'No, it can't be solved. If you possessed more than a handful of brain cells, you would have worked that out for yourself.'

As Essie watched the playback on Angela's phone, the

camera panned around the audience, recording the audible gasps and looks of surprise. Okay. It was pretty bad. Raising her eyes to Angela, she threw up her hands in surrender.

'Surely I don't have to explain to you, Essie, how completely out of line this was? The reputational damage from an incident like this can be huge. Not to mention, I had Anna Steenberger in my office in tears for half the afternoon yesterday.' Little flecks of spittle issued from Angela's mouth as she spoke, and Essie half-expected smoke to shoot from her ears at any moment.

'Steenberger is . . .' Essie hesitated, trying to quell her irritation while considering her next words more carefully. 'I was attempting to point out the flaws in her reasoning.'

'You could have done it in a less public and less humiliating way. Do you have any idea how much money the postgraduates bring to the Institute? Or how much we rely on the intern program to develop scientists of the future? The Board of Directors could see this, Essie. *I* should be showing it to them and showing you the door!'

Angela tugged at her skirt impatiently while Essie held her gaze. She resisted the urge to shrug her shoulders, instead clasping her hands together and massaging her scarred right hand. The skin between her right thumb and forefinger was always tight, and it felt tingly and slightly itchy when she was under pressure.

'This is only news because I am a woman. If Dr Elegan or Dr Wadsworth had spoken to a student this way, it would have been completely unremarkable. But when a woman acts in a way that is not sweet and submissive, it's a crime.'

Angela's face went red and her eyes bulged. 'That's a load of bollocks and you know it! I would haul Elegan's and Wadsworth's arses over the coals if they did the same thing, and quicker than you can blink.'

For a respected academic and the provost of the Institute, Angela had a mouth like a drunken sailor when she was in a rage. It was one reason Essie liked her so much. The other reason she liked her was because Angela was unfailingly fair. In a small part of her mind, Essie had to admit Angela would have reacted the same way if any of the other lecturers had done what she did.

'You only get the slack you do because of your expertise in quantum physics and because half the students come here to be taught by you. But this latest incident is the last straw. I can't trust you. I'm going to tighten the slack as of now. You are banned from attending official student events until I say so. Do you understand?'

'All right,' Essie replied softly, dropping her head to hide her satisfaction. No great punishment there. She hated student events anyway, especially since Cecil had retired.

'And you *will* make time to see Steenberger today to discuss her concerns and apologise for your tirade. Is that clear?'

Essie was about to protest about that requirement before Angela's steely look brought her up short.

'Yes, all right,' she conceded. 'Though why I have to be all friendly with her is beyond me!'

Angela pointed a stubby finger in Essie's direction.

'I'm not asking you to be her friend. I'm asking you to do your job and supervise her thesis. Provide mentoring and guidance. It's all outlined in your employment contract.'

'Fine,' Essie said, glancing pointedly at the wall clock to bring the conversation to a close. 'I'll get Ben to organise a time this afternoon, but I've got to get to my first-year lecture.'

'Good,' Angela responded. Her face softened, and she moved towards Essie's desk.

'You know I like you, Essie. I always have. And there's no doubt you're a brilliant scientist. I don't have to tell you that. God knows why someone with your potential wants to teach here when you could be at Cal Tech or MIT. But you need to learn how to work better with your colleagues, especially if you want the promotion. If the Board of Directors got a whiff of this internet thing . . .'

Essie winced. Why should her ability to work with others affect her chances of promotion when she was clearly the most qualified person? Teamwork was so overrated. If only Steenberger wasn't so sensitive.

Angela shoved her phone in her skirt pocket and folded her arms. Essie closed her laptop and fished her coat off the back of her chair.

'I understand what you're saying, and I'll fix it. But I've really got to go now, Angela. Can't leave the first years waiting.' She picked up her backpack and shouldered it.

'All right. I'll see you at the faculty meeting on Thursday,' Angela said, turning on her heels.

Ben ducked his head through the door as Angela left.

'Everything all right?' He asked innocently. Essie tensed. He had to have heard every loudly spoken word his aunt had said. He must know that everything was certainly *not* all right.

'Ben, call Steenberger and tell her . . . I mean, *ask* her . . . if she can come in and see me this afternoon sometime.'

'Okay,' he said, flicking out his phone from the back pocket of his jeans.

'Also, are you any good at internet video stuff?'

Ben raised his eyebrows at her and held up the phone that seemed permanently glued to his hand. 'I'm Gen Z. What do you think?'

'Great,' Essie huffed. 'That will make it easy for you to find out who uploaded that video of me arguing with Steenberger and get the platform to delete it.'

'Why? It has over twelve thousand views already . . .' he exclaimed, flipping his phone around to show her the footage again. The watch counter sat at 12,635. Essie scowled darkly.

'That's exactly what I'm talking about! I didn't consent to this. It must violate one of the platform's terms of service or something. Do some research. That's your job!'

'Okay, okay,' he retorted, rolling his eyes.

'Right, thanks,' she said shortly, shrugging on her coat. At this point, she would have agreed to be featured in ten articles on women in science rather than being a viral video sensation.

Chapter 3

David

David immediately liked the architecture of the Institute's main building. It was a beautiful sandstone structure built around the time he was born, making it old by Australian standards. As luck would have it, the photo from Anna's flat was the same one mounted in the reception area. It had a label underneath that read 'Dr Esther Thornton, Senior Lecturer in Quantum Mechanics.' Upon speaking to the receptionist, he was directed to her office.

'Good morning,' David said to a young man with dark hair sitting at the desk opposite a door bearing the doctor's name.

'Hi,' the man said, without looking up from his phone.

'I need to speak to Dr Thornton about a police matter.' David flicked open his police credentials and floated them under the man's nose. He looked up, revealing slightly dilated pupils. David detected a distinctive, earthy scent about him.

'She's at a lecture now.'

'I'll wait,' David said.

'Sure,' he replied. 'You can sit in her office.' He pointed to the door opposite his desk with the doctor's name printed on it.

David took a seat inside. There was a familiar scent in the room. He felt a prodding in his subconscious again, but pushed it away as an email notification came through on his phone. Morton had sent him further details about Dr Thornton, including a missing person's report on her father filed around two years ago. Skimming through the latest update, it looked like the case was going cold. There had been some early leads, but nothing had panned out. After almost two years, David knew it was becoming unlikely her father would turn up. His policing experience taught him the man was probably dead, likely murdered. He sighed. That had to be difficult for her.

David heard a door open and the air shifted, filling with tension, as a new scent assailed him.

'Why are you so wet?' The man asked.

'It's raining, you nincompoop!' A shrill, female voice responded.

'Oh,' he replied. 'I texted you. There's a policeman—'

'I had to turn my phone off. It started exploding with messages and phone calls during the lecture – all unknown callers. The messages were about that stupid video! But I don't even know how these people got my number.'

There was a moment of nervous silence and then an exasperated cry.

'Ben!'

'I'm sorry.' His voice panicked. 'But you're sort of famous. A journalist rang, and another person whose name I didn't catch, and I thought you might want to speak with them. There's also a policeman—'

'Unbelievable!' She cut him off again.

The woman flew through the office door, her glasses fogged with condensation. And beneath the damp smell of the rain, David picked it up – the scent of sweet cloves and plain soap. She dumped a black backpack down beside her desk then shrugged off her wet coat and flung it at the stand in the corner of her office. It missed the hook and fell to the floor. David cleared his throat and she spun around to face him.

'Who the hell are you?' she demanded, stepping back as she tugged on the wayward bit of frizzy hair that had come loose from her ponytail, trying fruitlessly to make it go back into the band. Her face had a sharp, distrustful edge.

'Dr Thornton,' David said, standing quickly and doing up the top button of his suit jacket. 'I'm Detective Sergeant David Sorrow from the Major Crimes Unit.'

She pushed her smeared glasses up onto her head and raised her face to him. He looked down into her blue eyes and felt the room tilt as he was thrown headlong into a stark memory.

It was dark. The road sparkled – the headlights of his police car bounced off the shattered glass – and a little girl's wailing pierced the night like a curlew. His heart clenched in response.

Refocusing, he realised Dr Thornton was staring straight back into his own eyes. That was always dangerous. Blinking hard, he extended his hand to her. She looked down at it and hesitated for a moment before she extended her own. He grasped it and felt the mottled texture of her skin under his fingertips. The memory sharpened and took solid form in his head. A green car, engulfed in flames. A man, unconscious, but breathing, thrown clear to the side of the road by the impact. A woman, a mother, crushed against the dashboard, no heartbeat. And a child's screams. Her terrible screams.

'Ben!' she shouted over David's shoulder, breaking into his reverie as she yanked her hand away. The young man appeared in the doorway.

'Ahem,' he cleared his throat. 'You have a visitor.'

'Thanks,' Dr Thornton snapped. 'I can see that. But what about Steenberger? Have you got hold of her yet?'

Ben shook his head at her.

'Actually, Dr Thornton, that's why I'm here,' David said, trying to draw her attention back to him. 'I tried calling your mobile several times on my way here.'

The doctor shrugged. 'I turned it off. I was getting too many messages about the video.'

'The video?'

'Yes. Didn't you say that's why you're here – because of Steenberger's video?'

David shook his head. 'I'm afraid I don't know anything about a video.'

She threw up her arms.

'I thought you'd come to investigate. Steenberger posted a video of me online and it's generated all these messages. Students do this kind of thing to teachers sometimes, but this is different. Some of the messages are quite vile.'

He noticed her lip tremble as she took her glasses from the top of head and used a corner of her shirt to dry the lenses, quite ineffectually. Whatever the video situation involved, it had clearly thrown her, and given the obvious link to Anna, he knew he would need to look into it. But the doctor did not yet appear to know anything about Anna's recent death.

'Perhaps if we might have a moment to talk, alone,' he suggested, ushering Ben out into the hallway and gently closing the door behind him. He invited Dr Thornton to take a seat in one of the two chairs opposite her desk.

'Dr Thornton,' he began carefully, sitting down beside her.

'If you're not here to help with the video, then what is this about?'

He stared at her a beat too long, the recognition of her face bringing him up short again. She was much younger then, when he had first met her on that rain-slicked road. Well, they hadn't technically met, so there wasn't much chance she remembered him. But her eyes were still exactly the same, those blue eyes that had looked so relieved to see him leaning over her in the car. His heart squeezed again at the memory of leaving her there, backing away. The pall of shame fell over him.

The doctor wriggled in her seat and raised her eyebrows at him expectantly.

David could no longer remember what he planned to

say, so he defaulted to a well-used policing phrase. 'I'm afraid I have some bad news.'

The instant the words left his mouth, Dr Thornton froze, her eyes locked on him but not seeing him. Her sweet peppery scent was abruptly punctured by the tang of adrenaline. He heard her heart kick up and begin to beat at double-time while the colour of her face turned ashen. Her hands began to tremble, and she doubled over, clutching her stomach. And he realised his terrible mistake.

'I'm so sorry, Dr Thornton. This is not about your father,' he quickly clarified, but it was too late. He placed his hand on her shoulder and she sat bolt upright, trying to shrug it off. She drew in a few deep breaths and slowly relaxed her arms.

'You're not? He's not . . .'

David shook his head.

'No, I'm from Major Crimes, not missing persons.'

He watched as she schooled her face into composure with visible effort. He cleared his throat and started again.

'I do have some other news, though. This morning Anna Steenberger was found dead at her flat. Her death looks suspicious.' He paused, waiting for her response.

Dr Thornton frowned at him and tilted her head in confusion.

'What? That's terrible.'

She didn't ask how Anna died. In fact, compared to her reaction when she thought he was talking about her father, her response was almost emotionless. Her heart stuttered out its usual rhythm, and she seemed quite calm.

When people are told someone has died, their usual

response is to ask what happened to them. David had come to see it as a funny thing that humans did to reassure themselves, as if knowing the mode of a person's passing was an insurance against the same thing happening to them. In knowing, they could avoid it themselves.

But the fact was, no one ever knew exactly how death would come for *them*. And dead was dead, no matter how it happened. Well, unless you were a vampire. Then it got a little more complicated.

'I am sorry,' he said. 'I was hoping I could ask you a few questions about Anna, though. I believe she was your PhD student.'

The doctor shrugged dismissively and crossed her arms over her chest. Her gaze drifted out her office door towards Ben's desk and she seemed to reconsider. Uncrossing her arms, she leaned forwards in her chair, her eyes intent on David.

'I'll try to help. What do you need to know?'

He drew out his notebook and pen from his breast pocket and flipped to a blank page.

'Do you know if Anna had any family or friends we could speak to? It seems she lived alone.'

She was thoughtful for a moment, a look of concentration drawing her eyebrows together.

'Her mother lives in Perth,' she said. David made a note.

'Do you remember the mother's name?'

She shook her head.

'What about friends?'

'I don't know. She was my PhD student. She was also employed to help me with one of the first-year classes, but I'm afraid I don't know much else about her.' She folded her hands in her lap and massaged the scar tissue on her right hand.

'You didn't pick up any other information about her personal life in the time you worked with her? Partner? Hobbies or interests?'

She pressed her lips together in a line, as if she were biting back her instinctive response.

'Steenberger . . . Anna . . . was in that video I mentioned before. It's not terribly flattering either for me or this university, and now it's gone viral.'

Her cheeks flushed. 'We weren't friends. In fact, I'm reasonably certain she's the one who uploaded the video. To humiliate me.'

David remembered the pitchfork drawing of Dr Thornton in Anna's cupboard. It seemed to confirm the doctor's words. She stood up abruptly and began pacing back and forth. After a moment, she stopped and planted her feet.

'You think I killed her, don't you?' she said.

Her scent was nothing like the scent he had detected at the crime scene, so this ruled her out as having been involved in Anna's death. Yet his instincts told him there was more to the situation than she was revealing. And he needed to go through the motions for the record.

'You're the only contact for her I've been able to locate at this stage. And it's too early to rule out any suspects. Where were you last night?'

She drew in a deep breath and appeared to weigh her next words.

'I was meant to have dinner with a friend, but he cancelled at the last minute. So, I was at home, alone, the whole night.'

David placed the notepad and paper on her desk and reached into his breast pocket to retrieve his phone.

'I was hoping to show you something from Anna's flat, to see if you could offer any insights.'

She looked at him sharply, suspiciously. He opened the screen and pulled up the camera roll. Dr Thornton reached for it, but he pulled back slightly.

'I want to warn you. These are crime scene pictures. It is not the victim's body, but you might find them disturbing, nonetheless.' He handed her the phone, and she grabbed it without hesitation, sliding back into her chair. She shoved her glasses up onto her head again and squinted at the images on the tiny screen.

'Those strange symbols – are they mathematical equations? Is it something to do with your research?' David asked.

She made no response as her fingers flicked over the screen, quickly scrolling through the gallery of photos. After she reached the end of the roll, she scrolled backwards. Pinching the screen, she zoomed in closer and then gasped.

David craned his neck to see what she was looking at, causing her to close the screen and hand it back to him.

'She has drawn me as the devil,' she said. 'Not very

creative, but not that surprising, either. As I said, she didn't like me much.'

She reached for a black backpack beside her leg, and he heard her heartbeat tick up a notch. She quickly glanced inside and then shoved it back under her desk.

'Do you know what the symbols represent, though?' He persisted, opening the screen and holding up the photo of the wall to her again.

She gazed off over his shoulder. Whatever she was thinking about caused her adrenalin to spike again, and the timbre of her blood grew rich with it.

'Dr Thornton,' he said, resting his hand lightly on her arm. Her face snapped back to his, and she pulled away as if he had given her an electric shock.

'No, I don't know what they mean.' Her bottom lip quivered, and she bit down on it with her top teeth to stop it wobbling. Her heart was racing at full speed now, her blood adrenalin-saturated.

'I will need you to make a formal statement, for the record,' he said.

'Can I do it tomorrow?' she retorted before softening her voice. 'Sorry. It's just I've got a lot of work to do.' She indicated a pile of papers on her desk.

He glanced at his pocket watch. It was getting on towards lunch time. There wouldn't be much harm in delaying until the next day. Maybe she would be more relaxed by then and it would also mean the forensics report should be available to him when she came to make her statement, in case there was anything else he wanted to ask about.

'If you come down to the police station tomorrow, we can do it there.' He stood up and grabbed his notebook, tucking it away again.

'Regarding the video, we have a cybercrime area that might be able to help you. I can put you in touch with them if you like.'

She laughed derisively. 'Can they block all the death threats?'

'Death threats?'

She shrugged. The thought occurred to him that the doctor could be in danger also. She and Anna had been related through the Institute. It wasn't out of the question that whoever had killed Anna might now target Dr Thornton for some reason.

He retrieved a business card from his pocket and placed it on her desk.

'Here are my contact details and the address for the police station.'

She lifted her gaze to his, and he could not resist holding it for a moment, despite the risk for him of prolonged eye contact. Though now a grown woman, there was still something of that little girl he remembered in her face: vulnerable, scared, alone. And in his own heart, he felt the heavy stone of guilt he had carried since that night. He wanted to comfort her, even as Rafael's voice echoed in his head.

We must remain detached. It's the only way to protect them.

'Most online harassment remains online, but it can be distressing. If you're worried about your safety or just want someone to talk to, please call me at any time. My mobile number's on the card.'

She tugged her glasses out of her hair and leaned over to pick it up. As she turned it over in her hand, he thought the hard edge of her features softened.

'I will come and make the statement tomorrow,' she said. 'And we might have some more info on Steenberger's family in the HR department. My assistant can direct you there.'

'Thank you,' David said, opening her office door.

'Hey,' she shouted. Ben took a set of earbuds out of his ears and looked up.

'This is Detective Sorrow. Can you take him to the admin building, to HR?'

Ben sighed. 'I was just about to go to lunch.'

Essie placed her hands on her hips.

'Fine,' he huffed, beckoning to David. 'It's this way.'

'I'll see you tomorrow, Dr Thornton. Just ask for me at the front desk.'

Turning on her heels without replying, she went back into her office, swinging the door shut behind her.

Chapter 4

David

'Ah, my old friend,' Rafael exclaimed as he opened the door to his apartment. Rafael's rich scent filled David's nostrils. A nutty aroma with a hint of sweetness, much like roasted nuts or coffee, washed over him. Human scents were as unique as fingerprints, but Amaranthine all smelled the same.

It was still early in his new investigation into Anna's death. When he returned from the Institute, Morton and the team were hard at work chasing down paperwork. Access to Anna's records. It was important, detailed work. But he had found it hard to concentrate after meeting the doctor. Or meeting her again. And Rafael hadn't returned his last message. Not that it was that unusual for him. The older vampire didn't think much of modern technology like mobile phones.

'Why do you not let yourself in already? The door is never locked,' Rafael said as David handed him the bottle of red.

'How are you, Raf?'

'I am well, yes. Come in, come in!' Rafael ushered David into the apartment and closed the door gently. His eyes glinted at the bottle of wine, turning it in the light to admire the velvety liquid inside, and he smiled up at David.

'This is very good, I think. Where you find this one? Here in Australia, *Dado*?'

Only Rafael still used his Croatian nickname. *Dado*. David didn't mind. It was a comforting connection to his past.

'I ordered a box online from Croatia last year.'

Rafael nodded, his silver eyes glinting. 'Of course.'

He went across the apartment to the kitchen and, reaching up to the top cabinet, he took out two beautiful crystal wine glasses and set them on the bench. Taking a corkscrew from the drawer, he twisted it down into the cork with little effort, but holding the bottle in one hand, he struggled to withdraw it, his strength suddenly leaving him. He cursed as an errant grey curl fell into his eyes and the bottle nearly slid from his hand.

'Here, allow me,' David said, rescuing it.

'*Grazi*. The mind is willing, but the body is betraying me at times.'

David swiftly uncorked the bottle and poured an equal amount of the wine into the crystal glasses. 'This body has served you a long time. You can't be too hard on it.'

Rafael gave a curt nod of acknowledgment before taking up his glass and holding the other one out to David.

They both inhaled deeply, taking in the many notes of fragrance in the wine. 'Bueno salute!'

'Salute,' David responded before clinking his glass to Rafael's and taking a sip, allowing the wine to rest on his palate a moment before swallowing.

'Is good, this one, *Dado*. Australian wines are wonderful, so full-bodied, but in this I can taste the mountains of home, the warm coastal air. I would like to have some of this for myself,' Rafael said, taking another sip.

'I can show you how to order it on the internet if you like,' David grinned.

Rafael waved his hand dismissively. 'You know I do not like these modern technologies. Come, sit. Tell me how you are.'

David hesitated. He would need to get back to the office soon.

'Come, sit,' Rafael insisted.

'I can only stay for a little while.'

'Yes, all right,' Rafael agreed. The two men moved to the old brown Chesterfield couch in the middle of the room and sunk down into its worn, studded softness. It was the only item of furniture in the living room, apart from the rows and rows of randomly-sized bookshelves that lined the walls, and a small occasional table, inlaid with mosaic tiles. Rafael's modest library held titles on everything ranging from ancient history to Jane Austen and published in many languages. They were shelved somewhat haphazardly with no order that David could discern, but he knew it made sense to their owner.

'I'm working on a new investigation,' David began.

'Is it one of these "ice cases"?' Rafael asked.

'Cold cases,' David corrected, unable to suppress a smile at his friend's slip. Rafael had spoken many languages over the centuries. It was entirely forgivable if he mangled an English word here or there, but it was still entertaining.

'No, not this time. This one is a recent case. A young woman died in her flat, not far from here. Although, as it turns out, the investigation involves someone from an old case.'

David thought back to the moment of recognition in Essie's office, when he had first looked into her blue eyes, the mottled skin of her hand as he shook it. He felt a tightness spread across his chest and he pressed his lips together.

'Oh?' Rafael inquired. He had known if he mentioned it, Rafael would be concerned. Encountering humans from their past could be precarious. Moving around every decade or so helped, and so far, they had both been lucky in Australia.

'It was around twenty-five years ago,' David answered. 'We were living in that little town down the freeway, do you recall? I had just graduated from the Police Academy. She was in a motor accident and her mother died at the scene. Car ran off the road. She and her father survived somehow. She was only a child at the time, too young to remember me at all.'

Rafael nodded. 'I remember the story. Terrible tragedy,' he paused. David could almost predict what he would say next. 'But we must be careful, now more than ever. The humans have so much technology. They can manufacture photographs on the telephones they keep in their pockets,' Raf said, running his hand through his thick grey curls.

David laughed at him openly. 'Raf, they can do much more than that with their phones!'

Rafael narrowed his eyes and leaned towards David.

'Do not treat so lightly with my warning.'

David lowered his head.

'You are good, detective. You have always been good at putting the pieces together. I chose you because of this and because of your – how do you say – *compassione*?'

'Compassion,' David said quietly, cupping his chin in his hand and rubbing his stubble.

'Yes, that is it. But you must not let your *compassion* blind you. If you want to protect the humans from the Bloodborns, you must not get involved with them. They are like the mist that vanishes in the morning sun.'

'I'm not "involved,"' David replied. 'It was a long time ago, and she doesn't remember me. The only reason I was even able to place her was the scarring on her hand. The vehicle she was in caught fire.'

He remembered the moment the electrical line overhead had sparked, causing the car to become engulfed in flames. Then there were more lights and sirens. He had had no more than a few seconds to make a choice.

David didn't sleep much, but when he did, he still dreamed. And that scene had played out in his nightmares for twenty years.

'This detective work is a means to an end, just as it was

in Croatia, France, the Balkans,' Rafael continued. 'You must not lose focus on our real quest. We seek the Bloodborns, and we destroy them. That is how you protect the humans. We play the long game.'

'I know,' David replied. He took a sip of the wine and swished it around his mouth, letting the fruit and cinnamon flavours wash over his tongue.

'But it seems like it's just the humans now, fighting each other. Homicides, theft, violence. I see no evidence of anything supernatural. Perhaps the Bloodborns have died out?'

'No,' said the older man. 'The prophecy was handed down to us from the beginning of time. For as long as they exist, we, Amaranthine, will exist also. And we are still here, in the shadows, waiting.'

David nodded slowly, regarding his friend's face. Rafael had a long, aquiline nose, dark, full eyebrows sprinkled with grey, and his forehead was lined with a depth of knowledge. He had been older than David when he was made Amaranthine.

David longed to believe that what Rafael said was true, that they were not alone. But it was getting harder with every passing day. It had been over half a century since they last encountered Bloodborn vampires and almost as long since they had met with other Amaranthine.

'Perhaps *we* will not exist for much longer,' David suggested, unable to hold Rafael's gaze.

Rafael let out a throaty bellow that shook his whole body and ended in a coughing fit.

'If you are trying to tell me I am getting old, please do

not trouble yourself,' he managed before another bout of laughter seized him. 'I have walked the earth for many human lifetimes, and as you know, I will not go on forever, not now.'

David frowned. Sometimes he could forget that Rafael was becoming mortal again, slowly and haphazardly. But he knew neither of them could ignore it forever.

'Do not look so concerned. It is the sacrifice of all Amaranthines – to make another, we must give up our immortal life. It was always this way, a necessary safeguard to prevent us becoming like the Bloodborns. Nika gave up her immortality for mine, and I for you.'

David nodded. 'I hope it was worth it.'

Rafael sighed. 'This is old argument. For many decades now you are angry with me that I did not tell you about the sacrifice before I turned you, but I regret nothing. Let it go.'

'We could be the last of our kind, Rafael. We haven't seen any Bloodborns in more than fifty years. And the ones we fought in Paris, you said they were not at full strength. Something was wrong with them.'

Rafael tilted his head and his forehead creased as his bushy eyebrows drew together.

'I do not think there have been other Amaranthine made for decades, perhaps a century. But there are others out there. Just as there are still Bloodborns. I feel it here.' He closed his eyes and placed his right hand over his heart. David couldn't be sure if it was true or just wishful thinking. He himself had never felt anything.

David's mind wandered to Orbost's comment to Morton about his ageless face, the source of his other nickname. He hesitated to bring it up, knowing how hard it always was to move on.

'It's been almost twenty years. People are beginning to notice. It's time again, Raf.'

Rafael nodded. 'I will start making the arrangements soon.'

Moving to the small window near the kitchen, David cupped his wine. The heavy drapes had been pushed aside, and the glass opened to the night sky, the bright cityscape visible from Rafael's top-level apartment. He stared down at the cars, floors below them, ferrying their occupants about their lives. Swerving this way and that, waiting for their turn at the traffic lights, headed home for the night. Or to a restaurant for dinner. Or to the theatre to see a show, or the gymnasium to play squash. On their own or with their family, friends, lovers. The myriad of little interactions and details that made up their brief existences, so trivial and so vitally important all at the same time.

'Do you think the humans ever really know, Raf? While they are alive?'

Rafael hesitated. 'Yes, some of them. Some of the time. At least a glimpse.'

'Aren't you ever gripped by the urge to run into the streets and shout at them, make them wake up? Make them see, while they still have time?' David asked wistfully.

Rafael was instantly at David's side, and together they stood, staring at the streets below.

'Not anymore. After all this time, I know Nika was

right. It would not change anything,' Rafael replied. 'They are always too distracted with the here and now. *È il nostro privilegio e il nostro fardello.*'

David nodded slowly and finished his glass of wine in one gulp. *A blessing and a curse.* Or words to that effect. He knew that Rafael was right. Humans struggled to appreciate the beauty of their lives until it was spent. He had been the same once. But while ever he walked among them, not quite alive but not really dead, he still had hope. In the end, what else was there?

Chapter 5

Essie

Anna Steenberger was dead. Essie turned this fact over in her mind as she cycled home in the growing dark. She would never pretend to be more upset about it than she was. That would be disingenuous. But it was still an awful situation. Dead, probably murdered, and not a single suspect in sight, except for her, apparently. The images the detective had shown her of Steenberger's wall had gnawed at her for the rest of the day. Why was she working on the Zion's Loop equation? It was completely outside her PhD topic. Essie had been careful to close the door on Zion's work when she published her dissertation, and she had succeeded until the video on the intern day. Why had she been working on it when she was murdered?

Dark thoughts seized her as the woman's cold voice on the other end of the phone echoed through her head. She had asked about Zion's Loop too, or rather, threatened. Could Steenberger's death be connected to the woman? It seemed too much of a coincidence to be unconnected.

Doubt had plagued her ever since she had made the choice to do what she did. It was the worst kind of academic offence and ethically compromising. But it had seemed the only way out at the time. Then her father had disappeared, anyway. And she had lied to the police about it. As if all that wasn't bad enough, now a woman was dead.

Maybe I should have come clean to the detective?

The detective. David Sorrow. She honestly could not imagine anyone who seemed less likely as a police detective. He was so different from any of the other officers she had met during the investigation into her father's disappearance. Tall, with a slight build, and pale, almost sallow skin. His manner was so earnest, his voice soft yet authoritative. There was something strange about him she couldn't place. His eyes seemed to change colour and when she looked up into them, she felt a tugging sensation at the edges of her consciousness. It was as if she were pushing up from under deep water, trying to break the surface, where the answer was waiting.

Or maybe the day's events just had left her feeling off-kilter? First Angela barging in and yelling at her for the video and then the news about Steenberger. The gut punch of thinking the detective had come to tell her that her father was dead. Her body was still aching from the pain of that almost-moment.

Arriving home to an empty house, Essie wished she were meeting Cecil for dinner instead. She lifted her bike up the front step and dug around in her bag for her keys. Unlocking the door, she wheeled the bike inside, leaning it in its usual spot against the wall in the entryway. She dumped her bag and shrugged off her coat, kicking the door closed with her foot. Her shoulders relaxed, and she caught her breath.

She felt like some comfort food, something her father would have made for her if he were still there. Unfortunately, she hadn't inherited any of his skills in that department, despite his best efforts to teach her. Her chest clenched again with the familiar ache of his absence. She'd have to make do with a packet of dried pasta and a jar of shop bought passata.

After she set the water to boil and tipped the contents of the jar into a saucepan to heat up, she opened a bottle of wine and decided to call Cecil to see if he was feeling better. But when she switched on her phone, a slew of notifications for text messages and emails bombarded her. She gasped at the first one that flashed on her screen.

Women should support other women, not vilify them publicly, especially in such a male-dominated field!

What gives you the right to be such a bitch to a defenceless student?

There were others that were not as articulate. If the abuse was this bad now, what would happen when news of Steenberger's death became public? Maybe it already was in the news? Would everyone blame her for that too? If only Ben hadn't given out her number. Essie shivered and shoved the phone in her back pocket.

A sudden noise from the direction of the front veranda

made her freeze for a moment. When she could breathe again, she tiptoed through the living room to the front door. With a shaking hand, she pushed aside the privacy curtain on the glass panel beside the door and peered out into the darkness. Nothing, no one. She lingered a moment before flicking the deadlock on the door and turning away.

As she headed back to the kitchen, she tripped over her bag, sending some contents spilling out onto the floor. Dropping to her knees, her hand closed over the little green notebook. She had decided it was too risky to record anything about her discovery on her laptop. The Institute's servers were targets for hackers all the time. She also couldn't risk one of her colleagues finding it. Once she had published her dissertation on Zion's Loop, she knew she could never talk about it again. But she had scrawled it all down in her own handwriting, to remember. She had chosen two identical notebooks and written it out long hand. One notebook she kept with her all the time, and another she had stowed securely in the back of an old filing cabinet in her office. She opened the book in front of her and flipped through the pages, her eyes travelling over the lines of equations, graphs and symbols, the only language that had ever made sense to her. Most of the time, she lived in disbelief about the magnitude of her discovery. Her scrawls on these lined pages were now the only record of that moment, the moment that had flipped the course of scientific endeavour forever. And flipped her life as well.

The detective's business card lay on the floor near her knee. She picked it up and turned it over. Something about him felt so familiar. Reassuring. *Call anytime*, he had told her. But that was just something people said. They didn't really mean it, did they? Nestling the notebook safely back in her bag, she took out her phone again and keyed in the number. As she stood up, her eyes snagged on the family photo she kept there. She stared at her mother's face, her beautiful brown eyes, so unlike her own. Then she caught a glimpse of her own face in the entry way mirror. Her wayward hair stuck out at angles and her cheeks were red and blotchy. *Esther Marie Thornton!* She pressed her lips together in a thin line and scolded herself. What was she thinking? She was behaving completely irrationally. What would she even say to the detective if he answered? It was probably just a cat or a possum outside. And whatever had happened to Steenberger had nothing to do with the Zion's Loop or the awful woman on the phone. It couldn't have. She shoved the card back in her bag and switched off her phone again.

A horrible smell hit her nostrils, and she ran to the kitchen. Pasta was boiled dry and burnt to the bottom of the saucepan. The sauce had bubbled over onto the cook top and congealed. She snatched the pasta off the heat and tossed it into the kitchen sink. Steam hissed up as she ran cold water over it. Flicking off the tap, she slammed her fist on the kitchen bench.

Enough. First thing in the morning, she would find a way to get rid of the video. Then she would go to the police station to make her statement about Steenberger. Once the video was dealt with, and she had finished with the police, things would go back to normal. She could put all these problems behind her and focus on getting the promotion.

Too tired to clean up the ruined dinner or think of cooking anything else, she grabbed a packet of potato chips and the open bottle of wine, lumbering up the stairs to her bedroom. She kicked off her shoes and flopped onto the bed. Stuffing a handful of chips into her mouth, she flicked on the TV and washed the chips down with a sip of wine straight from the bottle.

Chapter 6

David

After he left Rafael's, David went back to the office and reviewed the day's work before heading home late. Morton had interviewed all the neighbours, developed a working timeline. It was a good start. But he had struggled to concentrate on the case again. So he headed home for the night, hoping the new day would bring a different perspective.

His dreams were often plagued by memories, especially when he was troubled by something. He didn't need to sleep from a physical perspective. His body didn't require it anymore. But sleep gave the passing days more structure. A bookend to what was otherwise an endless stream of time. Tonight, he dreamt of the day the Ottoman forces had raised the white flag in 1913. The winter months that the Montenegrin army had laid siege to Skhodra were colder than average for a place so near the Aegean Sea, and the sun that warmed his face on the clear spring morning of surrender was very welcome.

But that was not the first siege of Skhodra, according to Rafael. David had met him in the queue for dinner rations that night. The man leaned in close as he spoke, telling him he had been with a small group of Albanians and Italians who had besieged the Ottomans on the same ground some five hundred years before, and lost.

'That is how I came to Montenegro from Italy the first time,' he whispered, accented with his native Italian tongue.

David scoffed in response. The man looked to be in his late forties, fifty at most. He was certainly on the older side for a soldier, but there was no way he could have been in Montenegro five hundred years ago. There was no way any living person could have been.

'It was unusually cold that spring too,' Rafael continued. As they chatted while they waited for food, Rafael continued to speak of that siege long ago, and David began to worry for the older man's sanity. Perhaps the long months of war and siege had finally taken its toll on Rafael's mind. He wouldn't have been the first soldier David had known to succumb to the dark recesses of his imagination in the face of a horror-filled reality. But when David expressed his concerns, and gently suggested he visit the infirmary, Rafael spread his hands effusively and grinned. A burley cook handed them each a plate of thin sausages and potatoes that resembled glue. As they took their plates and walked away, Rafael handed his rations to David, claiming he wasn't hungry.

Later that night, Rafael found David again, and the pair

huddled over a fire pit to keep warm in the still, snowy darkness.

'*Dado*, that is what the men call you,' Rafael said. 'But I think you have been called other things, no?'

David shrugged and extended his hands towards the warmth of the flames. How did this old man know so much? He wished he would leave him alone.

'My father always said I was a troublemaker,' David replied at last. 'I have four older sisters. All very well-mannered. I was the youngest and a boy. Apparently, I was always breaking the rules.'

Rafael laughed at this.

'But you are not a troublemaker. I have watched you. You follow all the rules, even when no one is watching.'

David shook his head and demurred. 'Not always.'

'Come with me,' Rafael said softly. 'I want to show you something.'

Lured by the mystery, or boredom, or something else he could not define, David followed Rafael away from the fire into the darkness surrounding them.

After that night, his world had never been the same again. Just like the night when he had met Esther Thornton.

Chapter 7

Essie

Essie swept past Ben's desk.

'You're late,' he yelled after her as she made her way into her office. 'I think I made progress getting the video taken down.'

Ignoring him, she dumped her bag on the ground and placed a pile of academic articles on her desk which she was supposed to have read. Massaging her temples, she tried to loosen her thumping headache.

In hindsight, consuming the entire bottle of wine, minus the glass she had poured in the kitchen, was not her greatest idea. She had slept fitfully and several times in the night she woke in a panic, convinced she had heard a noise downstairs. Around 2:00 a.m., she almost relented and called the detective, but after tip-toeing downstairs and checking the front door lock a few times, she got back to sleep in the early hours of the morning. But it was not the best timing for Angela Chu to burst through her office door again.

'Essie, we need to talk,' Angela said, her full lips coloured with a deep red lipstick.

'Angela,' Essie sighed, gesturing to the chair opposite her desk. 'Have a seat.'

Why was Angela paying her a visit again so soon? Maybe it was about the promotion? But it seemed too soon. Those announcements were usually made towards the end of the semester, or even the year. Angela's face was lined with a frown as she sat down. It did not look as though she came to deliver good news. She looked up at Essie.

'Are you okay? You look like you've been dragged through a hedge backwards.'

Essie moved her head up and down in a careful nod, trying not to induce a worse headache. She rearranged the stack of old exam papers and various yellow sticky notes on her desk into a neater pile and blinked a few times to moisten her eyes.

'Of course. I'm fine. Just a little headache,' she replied.

Angela opened her mouth to speak, but then hesitated, as if she were weighing competing thoughts. Essie met her eyes questioningly.

'What's wrong, Angela?'

'Essie, I'm sorry to be bringing you this news, but Anna Steenberger is dead.'

Essie slouched back in her chair and dropped her gaze. *Damn.*

'I know,' she said after a moment. 'A police detective came to speak to me about it yesterday.'

'You knew and didn't tell me?' Angela exclaimed. 'I just

found out from one of the Institute Board members who saw it on the front page today!'

Angela unrolled a newspaper from under her arm and flopped it out flat on the desk. The headline read *Institute Postgraduate Student Dead, Police Investigation Underway*. Essie pushed a stray hair out of her face.

'Sorry, Angela. I should have told you. I've just had a lot on my mind.'

'Yes, I know, the Induction day, the video – but Essie – your PhD student and colleague is dead and the police think it looks suspicious! I've been on the phone with them this morning.'

'I know, it's terrible Angela. But I think Ben might have had some luck fixing the video,' Essie offered.

Angela rolled her eyes.

'Essie, there's no *fixing* it. The video is all over the internet. I think it's called a meme.' She picked up her phone and clicked a few times before flipping it around. The screen showed a gif of Essie's face and the sound of her snorting in response to Steenberger's question. It played on a short loop, over and over.

Essie's stomach lurched like she had just tipped over the edge of a high peak on a roller coaster ride. The atmosphere felt thin. She went over to her office window and shoved open the sash, sucking in a lungful of fresh air.

'In light of everything that's going on, the Institute thinks – I think – you should take some time off. Maybe a long time.'

Essie took a moment to register what Angela had said.

Time off? Why? She turned to face her boss, her brows pulled together in confusion.

'You mean sick leave? I'm fine, Angela. I told you, I just have a little headache,' she inflected her voice, trying to sound upbeat.

Angela shook her head emphatically.

'No, not sick leave, Essie. Although you are entitled to that as well. You've barely had one sick day since you commenced your tenure. But I mean long leave, like a sabbatical.'

'A sabbatical? Why?'

Angela's eyebrows shot up. 'You seriously have to ask me that?'

Essie pushed her glasses up her nose and tried to concentrate. If only the darned headache would go away. Ignoring Angela's question, she yanked open her desk drawer and rummaged around for some paracetamol. She could have sworn she had a bottle in there somewhere.

'I've been fielding media inquiries and calls from concerned students since early this morning. Already several international students have decided to study somewhere else. Can't you see how much this bad press is affecting us? The reputational damage of the video was enough, but now this murder—' Angela stabbed her finger at the newspaper headline.

'Those two things are completely unrelated, Angela,' Essie said, giving up on the paracetamol and slamming the drawer closed.

'Unrelated? Can you seriously be that naïve? Steenberger is the student in the video. And now she's dead. Probably the victim of foul play according to the police.'

'You don't think I had anything to do with her death?'

Angela stood up and pursed her ruby lips before picking up her phone.

'Of course, I don't. But I've got a Board to answer to, who want to see the Institute full of fee-paying students and don't want this whiff of scandal about the place. You need to take a break and get yourself sorted out. Put some distance between this incident and your work.' Angela smoothed her skirt with an air of finality.

'But what about the promotion?' Essie asked, trying to keep the desperation from her voice. She blinked again half a dozen times and Angela narrowed her eyes.

'The promotion? Essie, that should be the furthest thing from your mind. I'm standing you down. Effective immediately. I have the Board's backing on this, so please do what I say. Otherwise, I cannot guarantee that you will still have a job at all when this is over.'

'What? I'm tenured. You can't fire me!'

'Read your employment contract. You have reputational obligations to the Institute. If you don't fulfil them, I most certainly can fire you.'

Essie grimaced and dropped back down onto her desk chair. After a moment, Angela's face softened, and she leaned forwards, pressing her palms on the desk.

'I'm not firing you, Essie. I'm standing you down for a little while. Take a sabbatical or even a holiday. When was the last time you had a holiday? It could be good for you. A chance to get over all the stress of the video and everything.'

'I don't like holidays,' Essie said sullenly.

This was all so unfair. The Board was overreacting, as usual. They weren't fit to manage a premiere scientific institute. They still read actual paper newspapers, for goodness' sake.

She reached for her coffee cup and knocked over the stack of papers, sending a few fluttering across the desk.

Angela leant forwards and gathered them into a neat pile.

'I want you to be out of here by the end of the day. I've asked Leighton to take over your first-year class.'

Essie was about to protest that Leighton Ellington was not competent to teach her course, but the stern look on Angela's face silenced her.

'Fine,' she murmured, dropping her gaze.

'End of the day, Essie,' Angela repeated as she left. 'Give your office keys to Ben when you go. You can submit the leave application later.'

Essie did not look up. After she heard her office door click shut, she buried her face in her hands.

How could her ordered life have come unspun so completely in the space of two short days? Her head was throbbing and getting worse as she fought back tears, but she would not cry. That would be the ultimate defeat. All her visions of the future suddenly narrowed to a small point that was the newspaper headline in front of her and a photo of Anna Steenberger's smiling face underneath it.

Ben popped his head through the door, and she hastily wiped her eyes.

'What?' she asked tersely.

'There's a note in your calendar about going to the police station this morning to give an official statement. I can't believe you didn't tell me about that yesterday! How did she die?'

Essie let out a long breath. A visit to the police station was exactly what she didn't need on top of everything else. But if she didn't go, she could risk making the whole situation at work much worse. She needed to be seen cooperating with the police if she was going to win her way back into Angela's good graces and have any chance at the promotion.

Ben loitered in the doorway. He had gone back to scrolling his phone.

'There's this one good meme, Dr Thornton. You should see it,' he said, grinning to himself.

Essie resisted the urge to throw something heavy at him. It wouldn't help her case to be violent to a co-worker right now. She got up with a sigh and grabbed her coat and bag.

Ben stepped out of her way as she marched out the door.

'Ah . . . Aunty Ange said you're supposed to give me your keys!' He shouted after her.

Essie pivoted on her heels and dug out her keys from the front pocket of her bag. She tossed them over her shoulder, and they made a clattering noise as they hit Ben's desk.

Chapter 8

David

David held the phone slightly away from his ear as Inspector Jefferson's voice boomed down the line.

'It's not every day a young woman is murdered here, Sorrow. And the Institute is a high-profile university. We need to make progress on this. Soon.'

'Yes. Understood, ma'am,' David said. 'We are making good progress. Don't worry.'

'Good. Keep me up to date. I'll have to do a press conference later.'

David agreed to email the Inspector some speaking notes for the press. He sighed as he hung up the phone. External pressure rarely helped investigations progress smoothly.

Gilbert Thornton's missing persons file was lying open on his desk. He flipped through it and stopped to look at the photo paper-clipped to the inside. It was probably the photo the police had used in the media following his disappearance. In it, Gilbert was standing in front of a restaurant with the name *La Fortuna* in gold lettering on the window. He was wearing a white chef's hat that sat lopsided on his head as he squinted at the camera. His smile didn't quite touch his steady blue eyes. They were the same blue eyes as his daughter's. The blow that had hit him after seeing Esther Thornton for the first time in twenty-five years pummelled him again. He pictured the Thorntons' green car, the front end wrapped around a tree. The first thing he had heard when he had jumped out of the police car was the little girl's voice in the night, crying for her mother. Then he had seen the woman in the front of the car, her chin resting on her chest. He would later learn her name. Rhonda Thornton.

The muscles in his neck tensed and he dropped his head in his hands. Maybe he should have followed Dr Thornton up last night? Checked on her?

He was so lost in his memory he didn't register Claire Morton's footsteps until she knocked on his office door.

'Sorry to interrupt,' she said, standing in the doorway.

'It's fine,' David replied, beckoning her in, grateful for the distraction.

Not for the first time, he noticed how pretty Morton looked. She had long, dark eyelashes and a smattering of freckles across the bridge of her nose. Her scent always reminded him of a summer's day with hints of jasmine and wisteria.

David had once overheard Morton talking with another officer, Denny, in the staff kitchen. Morton asked Denny if he thought it would be a bad idea to date a colleague. Denny had chuckled in response.

'You mean Sorrow? We all know you have a crush on him. You should ask him out.'

Morton never had asked him out, and he was glad. Being colleagues was not the problem. That was a normal human complication.

'Orbost just gave me the forensics report and autopsy for Steenberger.' Morton held up a manilla file.

David reached for it. 'Anything useful?'

'It confirms cause of death was intercranial haemorrhage – bleeding on the brain from blunt force trauma.'

'So, was she hit with something, or did she hit her head?'

'The latter, it seems,' Morton said, passing him the file. 'Her DNA was on the corner of the table. They didn't find any other DNA or fibres. The emailed copy of the report should be in your inbox soon.'

David's spirits sank a little. He had hoped some sort of physical evidence might corroborate the scent he had picked up at the scene, or at least offer another lead.

Opening the file, he examined the crime scene photos that Orbost had taken.

'It doesn't have the look of something pre-meditated,' Morton offered.

'What makes you say that?'

'The only injury is to the back of her head, no defensive wounds. It seems more consistent with an accident.'

David nodded. She was right. 'So, Anna either tripped backwards, or the killer pushed her and she fell. The killer panicked and ran? That would explain why the door was unlocked. They fled in a hurry.'

Morton nodded. 'Exactly. But if it was an accident, why didn't they at least call an ambulance? She might have stood a chance then.'

'Mm,' David agreed, closing the file. 'Anything else?'

'The data analysts are still sifting through the usual stuff – her bank accounts, emails, internet search history. The cyber techs confirmed Anna uploaded the video from the student induction day. I had a look at the comments on the video. Most of them are just keyboard warriors making noise, no one identifiable at this stage. We also got access to her social media. She didn't post much, but I did find a couple of conversations in her DMs with an ex. There were a few pictures of them together on her feed spanning the last couple of years, but it seems like they recently broke up. He was keen on getting back together. She asked him to leave her alone more than once.'

'Oh?' David sat up. A persistent ex-boyfriend was an obvious suspect, but there was no good reason to rule out the obvious yet.

'I have his name and contacts here.'

Morton passed him a Post-it note with the details. Jonathan Bradford. His address was not far from Anna's flat.

'Thanks. That's great work. Any luck with the mother in Perth?'

'Not yet. I've left messages.'

David sensed Morton waiting for something else, but he kept his gaze down.

'Ah, sir, after the morning briefing, we're having a cake in the kitchen – it's my birthday. Do you want to join?'

David frowned and didn't look up.

'Sorry, Morton. I don't really have time today.' He could sense her disappointment without looking up. 'The Institute's CEO was speaking to the Inspector this morning. They're very keen to find out what happened to Anna,' he explained.

'Understood. Of course.'

'But happy birthday.'

'Thanks.'

There was a beat of silence. David stood up.

'Let's do the briefing, and then I'll go over and have a chat with Jonathan Bradford. Can you and the team keep working with the analysts? I'm interested in seeing her bank accounts.'

Morton nodded. 'The whole team is on it. I'll let you know if we find anything useful.'

After she left, David flicked open the report in front of him again. The autopsy stated that Anna's time of death was approximately 11:00 p.m. The neighbour phoned in the discovery just before 7:00 a.m. when she had gone to ask for the spare key. The police arrived around 7:30 a.m. That was a big window. It left plenty of time for someone to make a getaway.

He heard Morton approaching this time, before the knock on his door came.

'Sir, sorry to interrupt again. Dr Thornton's come in to make her statement. They've taken her to the interview room.'

'Thanks, Morton,' he replied. 'Can you delay the team briefing for an hour, so we can do the interview now?'

David grabbed his suit jacket from the back of his chair and gathered up the rest of his case notes. He paused to check his reflection in the glass of his office door before making his way to the interview room. Standing outside, he watched Esther Thornton for a moment through the two-way glass. Someone had brought her a cup of tea and she sat at the interview table, holding the mug in both hands. Her hair, which had been messily tied back the day before, was loose and hung halfway down her back. Her shoulders were hunched and rigid. She seemed different somehow. He pushed open the interview room door.

'Dr Thornton, thanks for coming in,' he said, placing the file on the desk between them. She glanced up from her tea and nodded. Her eyes were rimmed with red behind her smudged glasses and quite blood shot. Had she been crying?

'Are you all right?' He asked.

She nodded and took a loud slurp of the tea and placed the mug back onto the table. Some of the contents splashed out, and David cringed as she used the sleeve of her shirt to wipe it up.

'Fine. Thanks, detective,' she replied.

'This interview will be recorded.' He indicated the two-way mirror where Detective Morton would sit with the audio visual equipment and a technician who assisted with interviews. 'Do you understand?'

'Anything I say can and will be used against me in a court of law?' she retorted.

'It's more for the official record,' he replied, wiping a drop of excess ink from the nib of his pen onto the top of the lined page in front of him.

'Following this interview, Detective Morton – who brought you in – will type up a statement for you to sign. Is that okay?'

Dr Thornton merely shrugged in response.

'I'll need you to say your answer for the recording,' he said, indicating the two-way mirror again.

'Yes,' she said sullenly.

'Thank you. Let's get started then.'

He asked her the usual series of opening questions. Full name. Date of birth. She straightened in her seat as she answered.

'All right, when was the last time you saw Anna?'

'The last time I saw her was at the Internship Induction, where the video of us was filmed.'

David asked a series of follow-up questions – some he had asked the day before at her office – and made notes. Although the doctor kept her voice even and repeated her earlier answers, she seemed more subdued than when he had interviewed her at her office. It was common to smell adrenalin on witnesses when they were being interviewed. Most people were slightly nervous in police stations, even if they hadn't done anything wrong. He couldn't smell adrenalin on her today, but she looked tired and distracted. She kept touching the side of her head gently and wincing.

'And you have no idea why anyone would want to harm her? Ex-boyfriend or partner?'

He knew he was leading her with the reference to the

boyfriend, but was hoping it might jog her memory about Jonathan or anyone else in Anna's life. She shook her head. 'No. She never said anything to me about a boyfriend.'

He decided to change tack.

'The symbols on the wall of Anna's apartment. What can you tell me about those?'

David heard her heart kick up a beat before settling again. She'd reacted similarly the day before, even though she denied it. She tilted her head as if she were contemplating her next words carefully.

'It looked like the Zion's Loop equation,' she said. 'I wrote about it in my doctoral thesis. It is, or was, a theory of time travel involving wormholes. But I disproved it in my dissertation. It cannot be solved.' She bit down on her bottom lip with her front teeth.

David's eyebrows shot up.

'You didn't mention this when I showed you the photos yesterday.'

The doctor shrugged. 'I was in shock.'

David made no response. She had seemed a little surprised when he showed her the photos, her heart had definitely been racing. But it didn't seem like she had been in shock.

'What does the name mean, Zion's Loop?'

'It's named for Professor Issachar Zion. He was a Swiss scientist in the thirties. He developed an equation based on Einstein's and Rosen's hypotheses of wormholes. Although Zion didn't call them that – he called them one-dimensional time tubes. It's my area of expertise.'

She smiled slightly, and he realised it was the first time he had seen her do it.

'Time tubes? As in time travel?'

'No. Not exactly. But it would have been a step in that direction. Unfortunately, my work on the equation, my dissertation, proved that the equation cannot be solved. Zion was wrong. It's a scientific dead end, essentially.'

She bit down on her lower lip with her front teeth again, this time bringing blood rushing to the spot. David tried to concentrate on his notes as the scent of it hit him in a wave.

'Did Anna work on the equation with you?'

She started to laugh before catching herself and then clearing her throat to cover it.

'No. I worked on it for my PhD before I even met her. She never mentioned to me that she was looking at it and it didn't have anything to do with *her* PhD research. It is strange though, because, as I said, it's a dead end. Although,' she hesitated, 'she did ask me about it in the video she posted.'

He nodded and made a note in his folder.

'And there's no one who can verify your whereabouts the night of the murder?'

She shook her head. 'I've told you already – I was supposed to meet a friend for dinner, but he cancelled. I cycled straight home from work.'

'No one at home? Partner, flat mate?'

'No.'

He noted this and replaced the cap on his pen, nestling it back inside his breast pocket. When he looked up, he realised that the doctor was staring at the pages in front of him.

'Your handwriting,' she observed, leaning closer, 'it's beautiful.'

David glanced down at his interview notes, rendered in the perfect Copperplate his mother had taught him at the kitchen table a hundred years ago, and hastily closed the folder. Try as he might, it was difficult to stop writing that way. Those curly capitals and cursives were simply muscle memory for him, but were quite out of place now.

'My schooling was quite formal,' he deflected, thinking about how to change the subject. 'That's all I need for now. Shall I take you to the cybercrime area while you are here? I have a colleague there who might be able to assist with having the video removed.'

She shook her head. 'No, thanks, detective. Ben said he got in touch with the video platform. He should be able to take care of it.'

Her face was hard with determination, but she didn't sound convinced. He was about to offer further aid, but she stood up with her bag and took her jacket from the back of the chair, so he opened the interview room door for her.

Morton appeared in the doorway.

'Can I assist with anything else?' she asked, eyeing the doctor carefully.

'Dr Thornton, if you go with Morton, she will type up the notes from the interview and then you can sign the statement.'

'All right.'

He glanced at her again. She was still looking peaky

and defeated. Despite all Rafael's warnings not to get involved, he found himself wishing she would confide in him and tell him what was going on. He wanted to help her somehow. It was a foolish notion. Even if he weren't what he was, he was basically a stranger to her. She had no memory of their brief past connection.

Instead, he said, 'Do you want another cup of tea while you wait? Or I could get you some water?'

One of Morton's eyebrows shot up.

Dr Thornton shook her head. 'No, thanks, detective.'

'Okay, come with me and we'll get the statement done,' Morton said, beckoning her.

David turned to go back to his office, not wanting to watch as they walked away.

Chapter 9

Essie

Mr *Linguine* was on the main street of a small shopping district, not far from Essie's house. It was not as cosy as her father's restaurant, *La Fortuna*, had been, and the décor was pretty generic. But at least the chef stuck to the traditional preparation techniques for the pasta sauces and they had a nice selection of red wine. Although her head was still a little too tender to contemplate any wine tonight.

Essie was accustomed to finding Cecil already at the table inside, poring over the menu, but it seemed he was running late. She tapped her fingers on the tablecloth reflexively and sipped her water. She took her phone out and switched it on briefly to check that he hadn't called or sent her an email to cancel again. The screen flashed with five missed calls and a dozen text messages, but all from unknown numbers. The influx of traffic in response to the video fiasco continued. Maybe Ben had given up trying to fix it after they had sent her home. She turned the phone off again and dumped it in her bag.

Seeing the detective at the police station, she experienced the same strange connection as the one she had felt with him the day before. It was the oddest sensation, like an invisible thread, pulling her towards him. As a scientist, she craved solid, measurable ideas. But every time she reached for the thread and tried to nail it down, it evaporated like smoke. The detective was proper in the same way as some of the older professors at the Institute, all suits and ties and holding doors open. But he didn't have the pretentious affectations of the professors. Except for his old-fashioned handwriting. She had been so absorbed by his swirling loops and serifs. No one wrote like that anymore. At least no one she had met. She commented on it to the other detective who escorted her out of the interview room and the woman had simply replied that everything about the detective was old-fashioned.

Since she left the interview, the reality of her academic disgrace and the prospect of long, endless days without a work schedule had been distracting her all afternoon. She was worried she would break down at the police station, especially when the detective had asked her if she was okay. But she had managed to keep herself together long enough to get home and cry alone in her bathroom. She would have still been there if she hadn't committed to dinner.

Cecil's grey head finally appeared at the restaurant door. He reached up as if to remove his fedora, except he wasn't wearing one. He stared at his own empty hand and then looked at Essie for a moment before a smile broke across his face. Essie rushed over and took his elbow.

'Cecil,' she greeted him, trying to take some of his weight on her arm.

'Essie,' he said, patting her arm. 'It's so good to see you. I'm sorry I had to postpone.'

Essie helped him remove his overcoat and hang it on a hook near the doorway. They made their way slowly to the table, with Cecil leaning heavily on his cane and Essie's arm. Essie helped lower him into his chair.

'Are you feeling better now?' Essie said as she sat back in her own seat.

He placed his cane against the spare chair between them. 'Fit as a fiddle. Just had a cold this week and the old hip is playing up a bit.' He patted his side where he had told her it usually ached more over the colder months. There was a sheen of sweat across his forehead and he looked slightly pale.

'Perhaps you should plan a holiday somewhere warm? Why don't you go and visit your sister in Greece?' Cecil's sister, Marjorie, who he called Mary, had lived in Corfu most of her adult life after marrying a Greek man. Essie had seen pictures of her house on Cecil's fridge. It had the most amazing view to the ocean.

Cecil frowned. 'I am too old for philandering about the world. Besides, who would you have dinner with if I weren't here?'

The real answer to Essie's question hung unspoken between them. It had always been Cecil and Sarah's plan to travel to Greece once he retired. But then Sarah had got sick, and after he buried her, Essie imagined all those plans seemed less attractive.

Cecil meant it as a joke about their dinner dates, but there was some truth to what he said. She knew she should try harder to make friends her own age. But she didn't understand how. There were social rules that didn't make sense to her, and it was too time-consuming trying to figure it out. She had other, more important things to do. But talking to Cecil had always been easy, ever since the first time she met him when he pulled his car over to help her change a flat bike tyre.

The waitress came and took their order. Cecil selected his usual pasta dish while Essie chose pumpkin risotto.

Cecil raised his eyebrows at her as the waiter left.

'Pumpkin risotto? Since when do you eat risotto? You always say risotto is just soggy rice, unless it was cooked by your father.'

Essie shrugged and ducked her head. 'Well, he isn't around anymore, and I just felt like it tonight.'

Cecil eyed her suspiciously and tapped his finger on the table.

'Out with it, Essie. What is going on? Did something happen in his investigation?'

'No. Well, sort of,' she demurred, pondering how much detail to share with him about the murder and mayhem that had recently overtaken her normally ordered existence. At least she was confident he would not have seen the video online. He didn't go on the internet much. So she could leave that part out.

'Well, which is it, dear?'

Essie let out a long breath. 'They found my PhD student dead in her flat yesterday. It's suspicious. As in, I think she was murdered.'

Cecil gasped. 'What? The red head?'

Essie nodded.

'I think I saw it in the news,' Cecil said.

Essie took a large sip of her water as she recalled the headline that Angela had shown her. Anna's face loomed in the front of her mind.

'Surely the police don't think you had anything to do with her murder?'

Essie shook her head. 'I had to make a statement. For the record.' It wasn't a lie. The detective had not yet confirmed she was *not* a suspect.

'Do they have any other leads?'

'I don't know. They are still investigating.'

The plates of food arrived at the table and Essie grimaced at her risotto as she ground a generous helping of salt and pepper over the top. She shoved a mouthful past her lips. Cecil looked at her in a knowing way.

'I think there's more you aren't telling me.'

Essie shrugged and cringed a little. 'I got fired.'

'What?' Cecil looked like he might choke on his food, and Essie immediately regretted announcing the news so bluntly.

'It's all right,' she said, reaching across to pat his hand. 'That was a bit dramatic. I've not actually been fired. Just *stood down temporarily*. A forced sabbatical. All the attention from Anna's death is bad for business. The Institute's business.'

'But they can't do that!' Cecil's voice bellowed. A man and woman sitting at the table next to them glanced over. Essie forced a smile in their direction without making eye contact.

'I checked my contract. They can.' She stopped eating and was pushing the rice around her plate with her fork. She finished the glass of water in one last gulp, wishing it was wine now.

'Well, you should fight them. Hire a lawyer. You must take a stand against this bureaucracy. They are insane if they think they can teach temporal physics without you. You are the reason that ninety percent of those students enrol for the Institute's course.' He was still upset, but had lowered his voice a little.

'Thank you, Cecil. I know you mean well, but I don't have the stamina for a fight at the moment.'

He hesitated before continuing.

'A sabbatical could be good,' he suggested tentatively. 'When was the last time *you* had a holiday?'

Essie raised her eyebrows at him. It wasn't fair of him to use that idea against her.

'You know me, Cecil. I don't really do holidays. I have my work, my house, and of course our little dinners. I like it this way.'

'But maybe it's time for your life to grow. Don't get me wrong. I love our dinners too. Especially after Sarah . . .'

Essie leaned across the table and squeezed his hand gently. He didn't need to finish that sentence. He lifted his water glass to his mouth and Essie noticed his hand tremble a little.

Their conversation moved on to other subjects, including the usual update on Moffatt, Cecil's Persian cat, who was involved in an ongoing war with a pair of pardalotes nesting in Cecil's courtyard. Cecil was a keen bird watcher.

'They are so tiny, Essie, like butterflies rather than birds. The most delicate, perfect things you will ever see. Moffatt will stand like a statue at the sliding door for hours watching them flitter about, then suddenly try to pounce. Silly boy always forgets the glass is in the way!'

Cecil's eyes glinted with laughter, and Essie couldn't help smiling with him. She felt some of the tension melt from her shoulders.

A waitress bought the dessert menu but neither of them wanted anything else. After a short argument, Essie convinced Cecil it was her turn to pay the bill. They made plans to meet up again the following week, same time, same restaurant. Essie bundled Cecil into his coat on the pavement. She waved down a taxi for him.

'Are you sure I can't drop you home on my way? I actually have something for you, but I forgot to bring it with me. I'm so forgetful at the moment,' he said.

'It's okay. I'll get it next week,' Essie answered. 'I have my bike and it's a nice evening.'

'I saw a new type of puncture kit at the bike shop in town the other day. Do you have a good one?' Cecil said, his face anxious.

'Yes, I've got one,' she said, patting the pocket of her backpack where she stored it.

'All right. Chin up then. I'm sure this will all blow over soon!' He said as he climbed into the taxi.

'Yes,' Essie agreed, even though she was far from certain it would. 'I'll speak to you soon. Bye!' She closed the taxi door on him and waved as it pulled out into the traffic. Despite everything, seeing Cecil had made her feel a little lighter. Swinging her riding coat on, she fished out her bike lock keys before rounding the corner of *Mr Linguine* to unchain her bike.

She hopped on, looping her helmet over the handlebar, and cycled into the laneway shortcut that would pop her out at the top of her own street. The laneway was edged with wrought iron fences, parts of it draped in honeysuckle, fragrant in its late summer bloom. She only closed her eyes for a moment to drink in the heady scent when the bike shuddered beneath her. Thump. A sharp halt. Then she was flying. Pain shot up her back as her tailbone hit the concrete path. A loud cracking sound jolted the side of her head. Opening her eyes, she glimpsed a shadowy figure in the distance. Ghostlike, almost shapeless. Or was it just that her vision was so blurry. Where were her glasses? Then there was only darkness. When she came around, she was sprawled on her back. A lady in active wear trying to control an excited border collie was hovering over her, speaking rapidly into a mobile phone, asking for an ambulance.

Chapter 10

David

David sat in his car parked outside Jonathan Bradford's flat. He wasn't sure how long he'd been there. There was no answer when he had knocked on the flat door earlier in the evening. He spoke to a neighbour who told David he thought Jonathan might be working night shifts. He flicked open his watch. Almost midnight. He should go back to the office. Or home. Try again tomorrow. But he was too restless for that. He leaned his head back on the headrest, turning over the details of his interview with Dr Thornton, struggling to push the memories of her accident from his mind again. As a police officer, he'd attended many fatal accidents, homicides and overdoses. Humans died. It was one of their defining characteristics. But for reasons he couldn't articulate, he'd never been able to get the Thorntons' accident out of his head.

He allowed his eyes to close for a moment. And it came

to him. The dream he had had many times before. The dream of the day he died.

When Rafael had first invited David to become like him, to be reborn Amaranthine, David had of course been hesitant. Although the older man had given many proofs of his wild story of immortality, speed and strength, David still doubted his own eyes. The war was all but ended. He could soon return home to his mother and sisters. He had even begun to miss his father after the long months away. Rafael's strange offer intrigued him, but he wasn't ready to give up his human life.

Then, without warning, the choice was forced upon him. While milling around the encampment as the army prepared to leave, a rogue enemy sniper, ignoring the armistice, fired into the darkness at him. A perfect shot. David fell into the snow, a searing pain burning his chest, his blood pouring out of him like water.

Rafael found him first, carrying him away into the cover of the forest. He lay him down at the base of a spruce-fir and rolled up his sleeve. In the delirium of his pain, David felt something warm and wet drip onto his cheek.

'Join this cause, and you will rise again,' Rafael murmured, holding out his bleeding wrist. Staring up into a starless night sky, and in the cold shadow of death, David had made his choice. As his mortal life flowed unceasingly from the bullet wound in his heart, his new, immortal life took hold.

They remained in the forest that night. David could not remember much of what happened to his human body, only that he seemed to exist outside it for a while. He recalled the sound of Rafael's voice as he gave an account of their origins. The Bloodborns and the Amaranthine, duelling enemies from the dawn of time. In Rafael's story, the whole of human history as David had known it was recast.

'It begins with an angry god, as so many stories do.' He spoke softly and fluently in David's native tongue. 'Enki was enraged because the humans did not worship him as he wished. He used his power to make *creature immortale*, not alive, but also not dead, a supernatural army to enslave the human race whom he despised. He named them his *Samanu*, the red disease. There were many more of us and them in the ancient world. The Old Kingdom rising in Egypt gave them boldness to come out of the shadows. We fought them . . . across Greece and Asia, while the ancient civilisations in Mycenae and Mesopotamia grew and flourished. Then came the great collapse.'

The next morning, Rafael handed David a set of civilian pants and a coat that he had stolen from the encampment. They were the clothes of dead soldiers, belongings waiting to be sent home, back to their families.

'What happened next?' David asked as he peeled off his uniform. It was stiff, caked in dried blood. His blood. But since Rafael had told him they would be deserters, they couldn't very well go dressed as soldiers.

'They came by sea, the Bloodborns. The Amaranthine were overthrown and the ancient world with them. Everything descended into chaos, but the Amaranthine regrouped and fought back. In Persia, the Bloodborns were defeated. They went silent for centuries then, and the humans again flourished.'

The Montenegrin army decamped, retreating, and David and Rafael slid away. David tried not to think of his mother and sisters, of the letter that would soon reach them, informing them of what he had done. It pained him to know they would think he was a deserter, a coward. He also tried not to think of his father, for whom he suspected it would merely be confirmation of everything he thought about him anyway.

He was enamoured of his newly acquired abilities, the speed, the endless energy, his body now seemingly unbreakable. When Rafael sent a hail of bullets at David's chest, he watched in disbelief as the last of the bloody wounds healed over, like sand in a desert hole, pouring back in on itself. Rafael chuckled lightly. His face crinkled with amusement.

'See. You are invincible to bullets.'

David shook his head and pressed lightly on one of the healed holes in his chest. There wasn't even a scar over the spot. 'But how? How is it I have risen from the dead and now cannot be killed?'

'Only Christ is truly risen from the dead,' Rafael answered. 'The Amaranthine are different. We are not alive, like the humans, but we are also undying, suspended in time.'

'What about fire? Extreme temperatures? Knives? The hangman's noose?'

Rafael inclined his head and smiled. 'I have been shot, stabbed, burned and yes – they attempted to hang me at one point. And yet, I am still here,' he said, spreading his hands expressively.

'As far as I am concerned, there are only two ways we end, *Dado*. One is if they take off our head, the other is because we become mortal again. One day, this will come to pass for me. And for you also, should you choose to make another Amaranthine after I am gone.'

At the time, David didn't fully understand what Rafael had meant by the last part. But together, they chased reports of the Bloodborns across Europe after the First World War. They crossed continents for over fifty years, following whispers and half-truths. Farmers stumbling drunk into a barn at night finding a slain sheep. Bodies found exsanguinated. Rafael taught him how to kill those Bloodborn they encountered, how to keep his blade sharp. And most importantly, he taught him how to cover up any evidence of the Bloodborns' misdeeds, to hide the supernatural world from the humans.

'It is better this way. Otherwise, there will be chaos. The *Samanu* will not risk open war with the humans again until they have regained their numbers and strength.'

He soon learned that though they were created as enemies to the Bloodborns, they were still like them in one respect. The Amaranthine, too, needed blood to survive. It was not the uncontrollable lust of the full vampires, a thirst that seemed to know no end, a hunger for blood they indulged in without remorse. But it was a necessity. Like humans needed water to survive, no matter how tasteless and uninviting it seemed compared to wine or spirits, the Amaranthine needed blood. Rafael showed him how to feed without harming the living, and how to not get caught.

'Follow a surgeon, or an undertaker, or soldiers into battle. There you will always find fresh sources of blood, without causing loss of life.'

David did as his mentor instructed, and with their speed and agility, it was relatively easy to feed undetected to survive.

But the world of the living no longer looked the same in his eyes. It wasn't the need for blood as sustenance that set them apart. Everything about his existence now placed him outside the mortal realm. He was not dead, but because of what he was, he could not truly live either.

'It will get easier, with time,' Rafael promised.

Would it?

David's eyes snapped open. Early morning light dappled the car's dashboard. He focused his senses. He could hear movement inside the flat above. Jonathan had returned.

He climbed the stairs to the second floor and rapped on the door. When it opened, a gaunt man, almost as tall as David himself, stood in the doorway in a pair of checked pyjamas staring at him blankly. His sandy-coloured dreadlocks hung to his shoulders. A tattoo of a snake was partly visible under the hem of his pyjama top.

'Are you Jonathan Bradford?'

The man nodded dejectedly, squinting into the sunlight. 'Yeah, I'm Jono. Who are you?'

'I'm Detective Sergeant Sorrow from the Major Crimes Unit,' he said.

Jono eyed him suspiciously. 'You don't look like the police. You look like a history teacher.'

David flicked out his police credentials. Jono leaned in to look at the badge and then shrugged.

'Can I come in please? I'd like to ask you some questions about Anna Steenberger. She was your girlfriend, wasn't she?'

'Okay. Yeah.' It seemed he was not entirely surprised by David's visit. Jono stood aside, letting him pass. David inhaled swiftly to catch his scent. He had a strong odour of stale sweat, cigarette and something chemical. He was obviously using some kind of recreational drugs. Or perhaps steroids. It was slightly obnoxious, but not the same scent David had smelled in Anna's apartment. Still, perhaps he knew something useful.

They went into the lounge room where Jono indicated a battered chair for David to take a seat on. Jono sat down in the seat opposite, legs wide, leaning his elbows on his knees.

'I am sorry to be the bearer of bad news, but Anna was found dead in her apartment two days ago.'

Jono's face crumpled and his mouth hung open in disbelief.

'What? What happened to her?'

'We're still trying to work that out, but she didn't die of natural causes.'

Jono shook his head. 'I – I can't believe it,' he said, pinching one of his dreadlocks between his fingers and twisting it tightly. He had dark hollows under his eyes.

'When was the last time you saw Anna?' David asked.

'Not for ages.' He sniffed. 'We broke up.'

'I see. When exactly was that?'

Jono's brow creased, and he began counting, using his fingers. 'It was about two months ago, I think. We went to the movies and then when I got home, she sent me a message saying she wanted to break up.'

'Did she say why?' David asked.

Jono shrugged and sniffed again.

'She said she didn't have time for me anymore.' He glanced at a framed photo on the coffee table beside him. It showed him with Anna. They were hugging each other and smiling at the camera.

'She said she wanted to focus on finishing her PhD. She was always talking about solving a really hard maths problem. It had a funny name.'

'Zion's Loop?'

'Yeah, that's it. Annie said she thought it could be solved, and she was going to prove it. Kept going on about it. Honestly, I didn't really understand. Maths is not my thing. But I'd tried to be supportive of her.'

David frowned. Dr Thornton had said Anna wasn't studying Zion's Loop for her PhD. She had also explicitly told him that Zion's Loop could not be solved, that she had proven it couldn't be solved. And she was the leading expert in the field. So why was Anna convinced she could solve it?

'Anyway, I went to her flat the next day to try to talk to her about it, and before I knocked, I heard someone speaking to her inside. It sounded like a man's voice. When

I asked her, she said it must have been the TV and no one else was in the flat.'

David nodded. 'Did you suspect she was seeing someone else?'

Jono scoffed bitterly.

'Why else would she just drop me like that?'

David nodded. Although Jono's scent didn't match the one in Anna's flat, he needed to rule him out by official means.

'Jono, where were you that night? Can anyone account for your whereabouts?'

Jono raised his eyebrows. 'You don't think I had anything to do with her death?'

'We're pursuing all leads at the moment,' David said, reciting the tired line that media training always told them to use during ongoing investigations.

'I've read some of the messages you sent Anna on social media. You were getting quite insistent about seeing her again.'

Jono threw up his hands. 'I was upset, that's all. I mean, I know we weren't together that long, but it still hurt, and I just didn't understand. I loved Annie. I would have done anything for her.' He began to weep openly. David looked around for a tissue box and handed one to him.

'All right, can you just tell me where you were that night?'

Jono wiped his eyes and dabbed at his nose.

'I was here playing Xbox with a mate.' He waved a hand towards a large TV screen in the corner of the lounge room. 'He ended up staying over 'cause we had a few beers.'

David listened to Jono's heart. It was a steady thump, thump. If he was lying, he was good at it.

'Can you write down your friend's name and number here?' David said, handing him the pen and notepad. Jono scrawled the details on the paper and handed it back.

'Are you gonna find who did this or what?' he asked. He began to sob in earnest, and David reached for the tissues, this time handing him the whole box.

'As I said, we'll pursue all leads.'

Jono took a fistful of tissues and blew his nose loudly.

David stood up. 'Thanks for your time. And again, I'm terribly sorry. I'll need you to come down to the station and give a formal statement, if you don't mind. Preferably today.'

Jono shrugged. 'Yeah, I can do that, if it'll help.'

'Good. Ask for Detective Morton,' David said, handing over his card.

He took out his phone and sent a message to Morton that Jono Bradford would be coming to the station, and asked her to check his alibi. While he was typing, the screen flashed with an unknown number. He made his way out of Jono's front door.

'Sorrow,' he said.

'Good morning, it's Detective Sergeant Sorrow I believe?'

'Yes.'

'Oh good. Detective, I'm Sally Donnelly. I'm a nurse at Central West Hospital. I found your card in the bag of a patient who was bought in unconscious last night. Dr Esther Thornton. Do you know her?'

David stopped walking.

'Yes, I do. Is she all right?'

'She was in an accident last night, but she's stable now. Do you happen to have any contact information for her family?'

'She has no family. But she's been helping me with an investigation. I'll come to the hospital now.'

As he hung up the phone, the familiar pang of guilt gnawed at him. What kind of accident had the doctor had? Was he right to have been worried about her safety in connection to Anna's death? He should have insisted on taking her to the cybercrime area. Whatever had happened to her, it was at least in part his fault.

Chapter 11

Essie

Essie's eyes focused slowly. She drew a sharp breath as she realised she was not in her bed at home. Yet the surroundings were still familiar, and so was the smell. Disinfectant and artificial fragrance. Soaps and hand sanitiser. Hospital. She was in the hospital again. Her stomach knotted, and she moaned quietly.

'Dr Thornton, it's Detective Sergeant Sorrow.'

Essie frowned, recognising his voice, and tried to sit up. Intense pain went searing down the side of her head and she winced.

'What happened?' she asked. A hand, his hand, was on her shoulder, gently easing her back down onto the bed.

'Probably best you lie still for now. You had a bike accident last night and hit your head.' She closed her eyes and her head lolled to the side. Why was the detective at the hospital? She moaned again.

'Doctor?' he asked, a note of concern rising in his voice.

'Why are you here?' she murmured, without opening her

eyes. For reasons she didn't understand, there was something strangely comforting about his presence. She felt the pull of his familiarity again. It was calming, despite everything. But she didn't know why. And she would never admit it to him.

'The hospital called me. They found my card in your bag.' He dragged a chair across the linoleum floor and the scraping noise made her cringe. She rolled onto her side and clasped her hands under her pillow.

'Dr Thornton, do you remember what happened to you?'

Essie cracked one eye open gingerly. He was leaning forwards in the chair, his pen and paper at the ready.

She opened her mouth to respond, running her tongue over her dry lips. He put his pen and notebook on the bedside table and reached for the plastic cup and straw sitting there. He passed the cup to her, and she lifted her head enough to take a sip of water. Taking the cup from her, he replaced it on the table.

She cleared her throat. 'I hit someone with my bike. I didn't see them. Or rather, they didn't see me.' Her voice was scratchy in her throat, and her head hurt as she spoke. There had been someone else in the laneway, hadn't there?

'Did you recognise them at all?' He asked.

'No, it was completely dark. I was on my way home from dinner with Cecil.'

'Cecil?' David echoed.

Essie's stomach tightened momentarily before she remembered putting Cecil in a taxi in front of the restaurant. He should be at home. Safe.

'Cecil Armstrong. He's a Professor Emeritus at the Institute. I worked with him for a few years before he retired.'

The hospital cubicle curtain was whisked back, and a nurse appeared, dressed in blue cargo pants and a matching blue top with the hospital's insignia on the pocket. She had cropped, grey hair and an air of brisk efficiency. She glanced at the tablet in her hand and then over at Essie.

'Oh good. You're awake again. How are you feeling?' she asked, her fingers flicking over the tablet screen.

During Essie's many hospital stays following the car accident, she had decided that nurses fell into two categories: the motherly, coddling types who saved you an extra serving of jelly or the ones who would not give you an inch of sympathy unless your lower intestine was hanging from an open stomach wound. She sensed this nurse was in the latter category. Well that was fine. She didn't need any sympathy. She just needed to leave.

'I want to go home,' Essie said.

'The doctor will need to see you first. You got a nasty bump to your head coming off your bike,' the nurse said, resting the tablet on the bed and picking up Essie's wrist. She placed two fingers over her pulse. 'It's lucky your injuries aren't worse, considering you weren't wearing a helmet.'

Essie heard the scolding in the nurse's voice and bristled. She usually always wore her helmet. It was just such a short distance from the restaurant to home. And everything would have been all right if the person in the laneway had watched where they were going.

'I'm fine,' she said, yanking her wrist free from the nurse's grasp. 'I want to be discharged.' She tried to sit up again and grimaced as pain radiated from the side of her head to her neck. The nurse pursed her lips as Essie lowered herself back onto the pillow.

'The doctor won't discharge you unless someone can take you home and supervise you for at least twenty-four hours. You have a head injury,' she emphasised again, looking pointedly in the detective's direction.

Essie swore under her breath.

'I don't need supervision,' she said, touching her hand to the side of her head warily and slumping back onto the pillows again.

She saw the detective exchange a look with the nurse. 'I can take her home,' he offered.

Essie opened her mouth to protest this arrangement, but the detective cut her off. 'Do you have another option, doctor? Someone else I can call? Cecil, perhaps?'

She wavered. She knew Cecil would come if she called, but he didn't drive anymore, and he'd be anxious about her, and she didn't want him to have to worry.

'No, don't bother Cecil.'

'Right then,' the nurse said, picking up Essie's wrist again. 'I'll take some final observations and see if I can find the doctor to fill out your paperwork. He's about to start his rounds.'

Essie exhaled loudly as the nurse took hold of her wrist again. She didn't want to go home with the detective, but she also didn't want to spend a minute longer in hospital than necessary. She'd already spent so much time there as a kid, with the burns treatment and skin grafts. If only the annoying dog lady had not called an ambulance. If only she hadn't been forced on sabbatical. If only Steenberger hadn't been murdered! A few days ago, she was an independent adult and a respected academic at a leading scientific academy with a promotion on the horizon. Now she was an unemployed, incapacitated woman relying on a virtual stranger to drive her home. Staring at the ceiling of her cubicle, she wondered how her ordinary life could have been so completely upended in such a short time. And why the detective always seemed to be in the middle of it.

Chapter 12

David

David stole the occasional glance at Dr Thornton as he drove. He was still analysing his reasoning for offering to take her home. She clearly didn't want his help, and he was working on an investigation, which was a probable homicide. He also hadn't completely ruled out the doctor's involvement. He sensed she was still hiding something. But it was the right thing to do, given she had no family. Especially if her accident was linked somehow to Anna's death. Still, he could already imagine what Rafael would say.

Don't get too close. Someone may notice. Protect our secret.

Physically, the doctor looked fine, but the discharging doctor had told him to watch her for dizziness or signs of confusion.

'Have you had any luck finding out what happened to Steenberger?' she asked.

'No, nothing conclusive yet. Although it looks like she hit her head on the coffee table.'

'So it could have been an accident?'

'Maybe, but more likely, she fought with someone and they pushed her.' He had no proof of that yet, but he was interested to see the doctor's reaction to the information.

She shook her head. 'That's awful. Steenberger and I might not have had the best relationship, but I do feel terrible about what's happened.'

David only nodded. His conversation with Inspector Jefferson played through his mind again. Morton had texted him earlier. The analysts were making progress getting access to more records and the team would be working hard to piece together the timeline of Anna's last movements.

'How did Ben go getting the video taken down? Have the calls and messages stopped?'

She frowned in response. 'He said he'd handle it, but, no, I'm still getting calls and texts. I've mostly been keeping my phone off.'

'Does your work know about the accident – that you won't be in today?'

She hesitated a moment, and he sensed her discomfort, colour rising to her cheeks.

'They weren't expecting me today. I've taken a sabbatical.'

'Oh?' He wanted to press her for more information, but she was staring resolutely out the window.

'Can we stop off on the way home and get my bike? Hopefully, it wasn't stolen overnight. When they were loading me into the ambulance, I think the dog lady said she chained it up in the laneway where I crashed.'

'Dog lady?'

'The lady who found me and called the ambulance,' she said. 'She was walking her dog, I guess.'

The doctor directed him to the top of a narrow laneway where he parked the car. She unplugged her seatbelt and fished out some keys from her bag.

'Wait here, I'll get it,' he said, putting a hand on her arm. She glared at him, but handed over the keys and slumped back into her seat.

It was an expensive-looking bike with a light carbon frame, chained against the fence where Essie thought it was. As David undid the lock, he caught a scent, the faintest odour of something familiar. Something long dead. He inhaled deeply, and his nostrils filled with the smell of the honeysuckle vine draped along the entire fence. It was almost sickly sweet in its waning bloom. Essie stuck her head out the window and shouted to him.

'The front wheel comes off,' she said, motioning to the bike. He exhaled. She clearly was not enjoying accepting his help. He unchained the bike and wheeled it to the road, popping off the front wheel with ease before angling it into the boot of the police car. He closed it shut and dusted his hands off on his suit pants, only to realise he had covered himself in bike grease.

'Sorry,' she grinned, still leaning out the window. He took out his handkerchief to wipe his hands.

As he turned the car onto her street, he sensed a rising anxiety in her, punctuating her blood with a tangy scent. It was a narrow road, lined with ornamental pear trees that had just begun turning their leaves in the slightly cooler weather of early-onset autumn. She directed him to a beautiful, two-storey terrace. He guessed it had been built sometime in the 1800s.

'You don't really need to stay,' she started, as they pulled into the driveway.

He didn't answer her. Killing the engine, he unloaded her bicycle and deposited it on the front balcony. He turned to find her trying to get out of the car. She wobbled forwards, and he was immediately at her side. She started and stared up at him, no doubt confused. He cursed himself. Over one hundred years as a half-vampire and he still made silly mistakes like that, acting on impulse. He offered her his arm, and she reluctantly leaned into him as they made their way up the stairs.

'I've got the keys,' she said, handing them to him. Her face suddenly went very pale, and she keened to the side. David gripped both her shoulders to keep her upright.

'Allow me,' he said, taking the keys from her shaking hand. Steadying her against the front wall, he slipped the key into the lock with one hand and turned it. It clicked open, but the door seemed jammed. He gave it a firmer push, to no avail.

'That's strange,' she said. 'Maybe the frame swelled up in the humidity.'

David put his shoulder into the door and, though he tried to be careful, it swung open with a clatter. The doctor frowned at him.

'Sorry,' he said, stepping through the doorway. Then he froze.

A scent unlike any other engulfed his senses and sent

him spiralling backwards – the rank, rotting stench of Bloodborn vampires. Though outwardly Bloodborns maintained the appearance of youth, just as he did, their scent was that of a decomposing corpse. It was as if nature still registered their undead status, undetectable by human senses. But it was unmissable for Amaranthine. Garish memories roared into his brain. Images of the Bloodborns he and Rafael had slaughtered in their journey across Europe and the handful they had encountered in Australia, raced through his mind. He inhaled sharply. His muscles tensed. Bloodborns had been there, in the house. Recently. The scent was still so powerful.

He stepped back outside, where the doctor was still propped against the wall. He should take her away. It wasn't safe. But she was not in good shape. There was a sheen of sweat across her forehead and her breathing was laboured.

'Sorry about the smell,' she said as he helped her inside and closed the door. He frowned before she said, 'I burnt my dinner the other night and haven't had a chance to clean up.'

'Oh,' he said, taking her bag from her and putting it down. 'I hadn't noticed.'

He helped her through to the living room and lowered her into an armchair.

'What a lovely house. When was it built? Around 1870 or 80 I'd say, judging from the panelling? It looks original,' he said, pointing towards the ceiling.

He took in his surrounds quickly while the doctor's gaze was drawn upwards by his comment. The house was messy, like her office. There was dried laundry on a clothes horse, bits of coal and splinters of wood from the open fire had spilled out onto the carpet, and old takeaway containers and teacups were on the coffee table. But otherwise, it seemed normal. Not like it had been ransacked at least.

'I . . . I'm not completely sure,' she said in response to his question. He watched her for a moment in silence as his brain scrambled to think of what to do next.

Rafael. I need to speak to Rafael.

'How about I make you a cup of tea?' he offered.

'Actually,' she said, 'I know what the doctor told you, but I will be okay on my own. Thank you for bringing me home.' She tried to stand up, but her knees buckled, and she slumped back into the chair.

'Dr Thornton, the doctor was very clear. You should not be left alone for the next twenty-four hours.'

She frowned at him, and he thought she would mount another argument, but instead she closed her eyes and leaned her head against the chair.

'You rest here, and I'll make you some tea,' he said.

'The kitchen's out the back,' she mumbled, without opening her eyes.

As he fled the room for the kitchen, he pulled out his phone. He dialled Rafael's number, but there was no answer.

Damn it, Raf. Why don't you answer your phone?

He quickly located the teapot, tea leaves and two teacups. As he waited for the kettle to boil, he disposed of the burnt dinner and scrubbed the pan clean. When the water was ready, he added tea leaves to the pot and retrieved a dusty silver tray from on top of the refrigerator, on which he placed the teacups, milk and sugar.

'Here we go,' he said, carrying it into the living room. He placed the tray on the little coffee table in front of Essie and sat down in the chair opposite her.

'I had forgotten I even owned that tray,' she commented.

'Milk or sugar?'

'Both. Three sugars please.'

David doctored the tea according to her instructions and gave it a stir before passing her the cup handle-first. Her hands were still a little shaky as she took it, and she nearly dropped it as she lowered it onto her lap.

'Can I use your bathroom please?' he asked, rising from his chair.

She grimaced as if she were in pain again, and then nodded towards the wooden staircase. Maybe the head injury was still hurting. He must remember to get her some painkillers when he came back down.

'First door on the left at the top of the stairs,' she said resignedly.

He made his way cautiously up the flight of stairs. Taking a quick inventory of the two upper rooms, he found the Bloodborn scent was all over the second floor as well. A chill ran down the back of his neck as he realised it was most concentrated in the doctor's bedroom. He flung open drawers and cupboard doors, not even sure what he was looking for. A different scent hit him, somehow piercing the veil of Bloodborn presence. He knew right away what it was, but leaned in closer to be sure. The same sharp, woody scent from Anna's flat. Not Bloodborn, definitely human. A sinking feeling came over him as he realised whoever had caused Anna's death had also been in Essie's house. Yet he was certain that the Bloodborns had not been at Anna's flat. Their scent was powerful, impossible to miss. So why had Bloodborns and Anna's murderer been in Essie's house? Had they been there together or at separate times? What was the connection between this and Anna's murder?

So many questions. But the upshot of it all was that as he had worried, Dr Thornton was definitely not safe.

When he came back into the living room, her eyes were closed, her head resting against the back of the armchair. David listened for a second and could tell her breathing had shifted. The teacup and saucer remained in her slack hand, thankfully empty. David gently retrieved them and placed them on the table. She looked almost peaceful in sleep. Her face had lost the edge of distrust she mostly wore and she resembled the little girl he remembered, trapped in the back of a car. Her screams came to him again, like a shock wave. The hard stone of guilt in his stomach almost doubled him over under its weight. He shook his head, battling the feeling away. He needed to stay focused. If he didn't, she could end up hurt again, or worse. He took a blanket from the back of the lounge and laid it carefully over her lap as he tried Rafael's number again.

Chapter 13

Essie

Essie awoke with a start, her body humming with a quick shot of adrenalin. She kept her eyes closed though, gingerly fingering the rug on her lap as she oriented herself, listening for the familiar sounds of her house as she tried to climb out of her half-consciousness.

She had been dreaming about her parents. Rhonda and Gilbert. They were at the beach, and she could smell the sunshine and see nothing but the clear, blue sky for miles out to sea. But then suddenly they were gone, and though she hadn't seen it happen, she knew the waves had swallowed them up and dragged them to a distant shore. She wanted to run into the water after them, but her feet kept slipping on the sand. She tried to call their names, but no sound came out of her throat.

Essie hadn't been able to picture her, but she knew the woman was also in her dream, lurking somewhere in her shadowy unconscious. A feeling of residual dread hung over her. She remembered the bell-like voice on the other end of the phone from two years ago, and it reverberated in her head, snaking its way down her spine like ice.

I think you should reconsider my offer, Dr Thornton. If you don't agree to work with me, something terrible could happen to you. Or to someone you love.

Footsteps on the front balcony brought her back to the present moment and reminded her of the accident and of the detective. The front door swung open gently and he appeared in the entry way.

'You're awake.'

Essie pushed herself up against the pillows.

'Sorry I nodded off,' she said. 'Thanks for the tea.'

'Don't apologise,' he said, making his way into the lounge room. 'You have a head injury.' He leaned up against the side of the lounge and stretched out his long legs. He looked so out of place in her house. But then anyone would. She hadn't had company over since moving in, not counting the one time a neighbour dropped by unexpectedly to welcome her to the street. She even insisted on meeting Cecil out at a restaurant. Looking around the lounge room, she clocked her dried laundry hanging on the clothes horse. The takeaway containers and other dirty crockery that were usually lying around had been tidied away. She felt her cheeks burn with embarrassment.

The detective didn't seem to notice her blushing. He actually seemed distracted. She stared at him for a long moment. The feeling came to her again that something about him was different. She could have sworn he had pale blue eyes when they met in his office. But now they seemed closer to an iridescent green. It reminded her of a churning sea. Maybe he had heterochromatic irises? It was hard to say from a distance. When he levelled his gaze at her, she quickly looked away.

'I went back to the laneway,' he said. 'Looking for any other clues about your mystery assailant.'

She felt the colour rise to her cheeks again. 'Well, it's probably me who was the assailant, but they did seem to appear out of nowhere.'

'Yes, so you said. I wonder, Dr Thornton, was there anything missing from your personal effects following the accident?'

Essie's chest tightened. *The notebook.* With everything that had happened, she had not checked her backpack since leaving the restaurant. She eyed the bag, still lying in the entryway.

'Do you think they would have robbed me while I was out cold? The dog lady did not seem the type.'

David chuckled. 'Perhaps not her, but maybe the person you collided with?'

Essie frowned. Whoever they were, they should have come off worse than her. She had hit them with her bike. Still, doubt nagged at her.

'Can you pass me my bag over there?'

He retrieved it from the entryway and placed it on Essie's lap. She unzipped it carefully and took out her laptop, wallet, phone and a small makeup case, laying them out on the coffee table. She looked inside it again and felt around the bottom.

'Oh no,' she breathed, unable to conceal her reaction.

'Is something wrong, Dr Thornton?'

She contemplated lying for a split second, then decided that it would probably draw more suspicion than telling the truth. 'It's my notebook. It's gone,' she said.

'What do you have a notebook for? I thought everything was computerised these days. Especially for scientists.'

Why would a mugger in the laneway have stolen the notebook? It didn't make any sense. Assuming they were an opportunistic thief, why would they have taken it and left more valuable items – her laptop, wallet and phone? It was a perfectly ordinary looking book with lined pages. That was why she had used it. And the entries would be indecipherable to the untrained eye. Lines of code and equations. Essie felt the room closing in on her.

'I mostly use my laptop for work, but I had some other . . . handwritten notes. About the Zion's Loop equation. Research I did for my dissertation. It was easier to scribble them down on paper.'

'I see,' said David, looking unconvinced. 'Why were you still carrying that around? I thought you published your dissertation years ago?'

Essie put the bag down and pressed her fingers against her temples, trying hard not to hyperventilate. Perhaps the book had fallen out at work or at the hospital? Even as she had the thought, she knew it was unlikely. She always kept the bag zipped up for exactly that reason. She was very careful about it. How could she impress on the detective the importance of the book without alerting him to the contents? He likely wouldn't understand, even if she tried to explain. What if the book had gotten into the wrong hands? She heard the woman's voice in head again, child-like and chilling, and shivered.

'Dr Thornton?' The detective was watching her, his face concerned. She felt his hand rest lightly on her shoulder. 'Are you cold?'

She slowly shook her head side to side, trying to catch her breath, but it was already coming too fast and shallow to control. The room tilted on an axis and she clutched the arm of the chair for support.

The detective frowned. 'Perhaps you should go upstairs and lie down for a while?'

'But what about my notebook?' she protested.

'When you're feeling better, I will take you to make a stolen goods report.'

She didn't want to admit it, but the detective's words made her feel marginally calmer. Maybe the notebook was just that – stolen goods? Whoever took it would open it up and realise it was a string of useless numbers and symbols and throw it in the bin. And it *was* next to useless without the other half, which should still be locked away in her office. Ben had taken her keys. No one could get in there. What else could she do anyway, given the circumstances? She could hardly go out looking for the book herself. She could barely hold up her own head, and the detective would be unlikely to let her leave the house. Whatever had happened to the notebook, and whoever now possessed it, she was in no fit state to pursue it. She nodded her agreement to his suggestion and stood up to go to her bedroom, swaying a little on her feet.

'Do you want me to help you?' He offered her his arm.

'No,' she said sharply, then added more softly, 'I'll be all right.' She knew he didn't intend her any harm, but the last thing she needed was this man invading any more of her personal space. Maybe a good night's sleep would clear her head so that tomorrow morning she could come up with an actual plan to find the book.

He stepped back.

'Very well. I'll stay here tonight. Doctor's orders.' He smiled at her, but she grimaced reflexively.

'You don't need to. I'm sure I'll be fine,' she said.

'Doctor's orders,' he repeated in a way that did not invite dispute. The room tilted again, and she grabbed the handrail for support. Breathless and dizzy, she didn't have what it took to argue further.

'All right. I hope you like sleeping on couches,' she said, waving in the direction of the small one in her lounge room. He was far too tall for it. His legs would hang over the end by at least half a metre. But if he insisted on staying, then that was all she could offer.

'There are some blankets in there.' She pointed to the cupboard near the entryway.

He nodded. 'Sleep well, Dr Thornton.'

Leaning against the handrail for support at each tread, she made her way up the stairs and along the hallway to her bedroom. She toed off her shoes and crawled under the quilt, not caring that she was still in the clothes she had been wearing since yesterday. Turning on her side, she stared at the photo of her and her father she kept on her nightstand. She was standing next to him in the kitchen at his restaurant, propped up on a stool so she could reach the bench. There was a dab of flour on her nose and her father's hands were clasped over hers, guiding her, showing her how to fold the dough. He had always been there for her, supported her work even when he could barely understand half of it. She had tried for two years to push the thought from her mind, hoping against hope that he had just packed up one day and decided to take a break. But in her heart, she knew he'd never have left without saying goodbye. No, this was all her fault. Even though she had tried to prevent it, that woman had probably made good on her threats, and now it was too late. She reached out with her scarred hand to touch his photo-face, and felt her chest constrict.

Where are you, Dad? I need you.

She imagined being enfolded in his bear-like hug, inhaling the aroma that was uniquely his, kind of earthy. Letting out a long sigh, she pulled the quilt around her. Sleep came over her warmly and she surrendered to it.

Chapter 14

David

David paced the doctor's lounge room, his phone up to his ear, dialling Rafael's number for the tenth time. Finally, he heard the click as his call was answered.

'Hello,' Rafael croaked.

'Raf, I've been calling you for hours!' David almost shouted, before remembering Dr Thornton was upstairs, hopefully asleep. 'Did you get my message?'

'I am sorry. I have been sick. First time in over four centuries I am sick. I forgot how unpleasant it is.'

'What? You can't get sick. We don't get sick,' David replied.

'My time began to end when I made you. This body is becoming human again, with all its frailty.' As if to emphasise the point, Rafael choked out a loud, phlegmy cough.

David's heart sank. He knew his friend would recover from this cold. But it was another symptom of things to come. Rafael's once invincible body was slowly decaying.

Little chinks in his armour were emerging. The process was not systematic, and he could go years without any change. Then suddenly he would be struck with arthritis in his hands for a month and the next month he would be completely fine again. But the overall trajectory was heading in a downwards direction. Like a fluorescent light tube that flashes intermittently when it's degrading before finally blinking out. One day Rafael would blink out and David would be alone. Unless he made another like himself. He pushed those thoughts aside as his mind returned to the current dilemma.

'I'm sorry you've been unwell, but I need your help. This case I have – the one with the woman I met years ago. The Bloodborns are involved. One or more were in her house yesterday or even last night.'

Rafael's reply was short. 'I am coming. Where are you?'

He gave Rafael Dr Thornton's address and hung up the phone.

He had gone back and scoured every inch of the laneway. The Bloodborns' scent was fainter in the outdoors and the honeysuckle perfume had partially masked it. But there was no doubt in his mind now that they had been in the house and in the laneway. They probably caused the bike accident too. But why attack the doctor there, out in the open, when they knew where she lived? And if a Bloodborn was after her, why was she still alive?

The same human who caused Anna's death had been in the doctor's house, but so had a vampire. It all seemed too unlikely to be a coincidence. Somehow, it all had to be connected, but he was struggling to pull the threads together. And Dr Thornton had become quite worked up over a stolen notebook. He had smelt the adrenalin kick into her bloodstream when she made the discovery it was gone. The sense of doubt that had crept over him at his first meeting with her flooded back to him. Her distrust, her guardedness. There was something she didn't want him to know.

What wasn't she telling him? And how could he get her to open up?

He stood at the bottom of her stairs and listened for a moment, detecting the sound of her soft breaths, in and out. At least she was sleeping again. He was clearing the teacups and tea pot away in the kitchen when he heard a soft click and felt a rush of cool air beside him. Rafael's spiced scent washed over him.

'You seem to have figured out the front door. I practically had to rip it open.' Now that he stopped to think about it, the stuck door should have been a clue. Likely it was broken by the intruder.

'Who says I came in the front door?' Rafael smirked, and then cocked his head to the side as if he had heard a noise. 'Fresh, very fresh,' he sighed, his lids sliding closed as he inhaled deeply. 'You are right. They were here not long ago.'

He opened his eyes and settled his gaze on David.

'Come, my friend. Tell me everything.'

They sat in the armchairs in the lounge room while David rapidly recounted the events of the last twenty-four hours and how he'd come to be in the doctor's house.

'Whoever murdered Anna Steenberger has been here in this house too. Somehow these two cases are linked.'

'And you say the scents are most concentrated upstairs, in her bedroom?' Rafael said, casting his gaze towards the staircase.

'Yes. But there's more. I'm fairly certain the bike accident wasn't an accident at all. The Bloodborns were in the laneway where the doctor crashed.'

Rafael rested his elbows on his knees and tented his fingers together in front of him.

'The doctor seems to be at the centre of all this, but what is it that makes her special?'

David shrugged. 'She worked with Anna. And as you know, I met the doctor once, long ago. Other than that, I don't know.'

Rafael hesitated a moment as he fingered the buttons of his coat. He raised an eyebrow at David.

'Unless she has been working with the Bloodborns? I have known many humans who have turned on their own kind. The promise of immortality is very attractive to those who have not experienced it.'

'What?' David half yelled, before tempering the volume of his voice again to a low whisper.

'The Bloodborns have been all over her house and attacked her in the street, but she lives. You know their nature. Humans are disposable. So why is she still breathing?'

'No,' David said firmly. Despite the gnawing doubt about her that was playing at the edge of his

106

consciousness, he still didn't believe she was helping the Bloodborns. It didn't make sense.

'If she was working with them, why would they attack her?'

'Maybe they wish to sow doubt and chaos or to lure us here into a trap? They are the children of Enki. It is what they do.'

David just shook his head again. Rafael sat motionless, meeting his gaze.

'We have talked about this, my friend. You become too attached to the humans. And with this woman, you also feel so much guilt because of the accident. You could not protect her then, so you want to make sure you do now. It is noble, it is very like you, but it is clouding your judgement.'

David bristled. He knew Rafael's words came from good intentions. It was the only way. To protect the human world, for the greater good, sometimes it came at the cost of individual lives. It's why they had to sit outside humanity, to ride the wave of time as it rolled onwards. Human attachments were like anchors. On the great sea of time, anchors were the death knell. Staying anchored could break a ship apart. To survive the stormy seas, they had to stay fluid and agile, floating along the top.

'I understand what you're saying, Raf, but I honestly don't think she knows anything. She panicked tonight about a notebook. I think the Bloodborns took it from her while she was unconscious. I need to figure out why.'

Rafael shrugged and nodded his head.

'There were no Bloodborns in Anna Steenberger's flat. You are certain of this?'

Rafael's question put doubt into David's mind. Maybe he had overlooked something? The Bloodborns' scent was unmistakable, but he had missed it the first time in the laneway. And Rafael had a point. It didn't make sense they had been at the doctor's house and not at the crime scene.

His face must have betrayed his uncertainty.

'I will return to Anna's flat to check.'

Glancing up at Rafael, David noticed his friend's brow was beading with sweat.

'You should go home and get some more rest. I'll let you know what I find out, and we can regroup tomorrow.'

'No,' Rafael said. 'I should stay. What if they return?'

David smoothed his hair in place and shrugged.

'Listen, Dr Thornton will be suspicious if she finds you here. I'll have no chance of finding out about the notebook if her guard is up. Stay by your phone. I'll call you if anything happens.'

'It has been so long since we hunted them, you have forgotten their speed, their strength. You will not have time to make any calls if a Bloodborn is here,' Rafael laughed, then the laughter dissolved into a throaty cough that doubled him over.

David patted him on the back gently. The older man leaned on David's shoulder and held his gaze level.

'Have you drunk today?'

David nodded. 'This morning, before I left home.' It was refrigerated, days old blood from the blood bank, but it did the job.

Rafael looked pleased. 'That will help keep your strength. They drink all the time and from living victims. The blood from the vein is . . . how you say . . . *più potente*?'

'More powerful. I know,' David said. Rafael's face grew anxious.

'I will check Anna's flat now. Send me the address. I won't be long.' Rafael walked to the front door and reached for the handle before he turned back. His hand bristled across his bearded chin before he spoke.

'You made a hard choice when you left the girl in the burning car. But you kept your vow. For the sake of all humanity, there are sometimes sacrifices. If you revealed yourself to the humans that night . . .'

David frowned. Part of him thought Rafael was right. But his words also provoked the question that had so troubled David's conscience the past twenty-five years. A question, if he was honest, that had troubled him from the beginning.

'What if I chose wrongly though? What if protecting all humanity means nothing without being able to protect that one person right in front of us?'

Rafael drew a long breath and sighed it out again.

'I will be back,' he said, and then, with a light swish of the air, he was gone.

Chapter 15

Essie

Essie opened her eyes slowly, struggling to adjust to the darkness and find the familiar outlines of her bedroom. She swallowed against her dry throat and realised she had slept quite soundly. Maybe having the detective in her house had settled her nerves. There were no bad dreams, no startling awake at strange noises. Only the need for the toilet had woken her now.

Fumbling her way along the hallway as she put her glasses on, she reached the bathroom door and flicked the light switch on. When she was finished, she washed her hands and slurped a mouthful of water from the tap, swishing it around to moisten her throat. She dried her hands and turned off the light.

A hint of movement in the hall flittered in her peripheral vision, and she turned her head towards her office door. Although the room was pitch black, she sensed a darker shadow hovering near the bookshelf. Perhaps the detective had had trouble sleeping and come upstairs to find a book? But why was he looking with the light off? She moved towards the doorway and reached for the switch.

Before she could flick the light on, the shadowy figure rushed towards her quickly, nearly too quickly to make sense, a flash of silver. She screamed as she lost her balance, falling backwards against the hallway wall with a thud. She felt another presence beside her and jumped as it grabbed her arm, pulling her away.

'Stay back!' It was the detective.

Before she could answer, the shadow rushed out of the office door and the detective launched himself at it. There was a loud crashing noise, like an explosion, and a scrape of metal on the wooden floor. Though Essie could hardly make out what was happening in the darkness, it seemed the detective was wrestling with the other figure.

A grunt, followed by a growling sound, animalistic, came from the melee. Essie instinctively took several steps back. Her eyes, adjusting to the low light, could just make out the intruder as they turned in her direction, growling and baring a row of teeth, that gleamed in the darkness. She narrowed her eyes, confusion raging between what she thought she was seeing and what her brain could understand. The intruder seemed to be a middle-aged man, broad-shouldered and slightly stocky. His lips were pulled back in a snarl, revealing long incisor teeth that looked like . . . fangs. There was no other way to describe it. Essie frowned and shook herself in disbelief. Maybe hitting her head had brought on more than a slight concussion? Maybe she had a full-on brain injury?

She fumbled for the hall light switch and flipped it on.

The man flinched and shielded his eyes from the sudden illumination. The detective used the distraction to flip him over, pinning him to the ground. He managed to hold him down for a moment before, in one fluid movement, the intruder kicked him off, sending the detective flying into the wall with a sickening crack. A shower of gyprock and wooden splinters rained down onto the floor. There was a metallic glint as the man plunged something into the detective's limp body.

Essie's hand flew to her mouth as she tried to scream again. This time no sound came out. How had that man been able to do that? It sounded as though he had broken the detective's back or cracked his head open. And then he had stabbed him in the chest. Her breath caught in her throat. The detective must be dead. There was no way he could have survived that. The man straightened up and spun around. As he stalked in her direction, his eyes captured Essie's attention and she stared at them in open-mouthed horror. Abnormally large and rounded, they were rimmed in a vibrant red colour, the irises as black as coal, the whites threaded with reedy veins.

The man held up the shiny object as he advanced on Essie. It was a sharp looking blade. Her eyes fell on a marble doorstop holding the office door open, but she doubted she could lift or throw it with enough force to be useful. Her only chance was to run to her room and lock the door, even though after what she had seen, she was doubtful a locked door would help much. She moved backwards up the hallway, not taking her eyes from the man. His eerie gaze tracked her every step like a homing beacon. She backed into the doorframe of her room and reached for the handle with a shaking hand. But the intruder just *disappeared*. It wasn't that he left quickly. It wasn't that she turned away briefly and then he was gone. He was there, in the hallway, right in front of her, and then he vanished.

She took a couple of tentative steps towards the crater in the wall, her legs wobbling, expecting to see the detective lying unconscious there. But he too was gone. There were several drops of blood on the floor, but the hole in the wall was empty. She leaned back against the opposite wall to steady herself and found her knees giving way. Sliding slowly down to the floorboards, she closed her eyes as lights danced behind her eyelids.

Am I going to pass out? I think I might pass out.

She focused on trying to slow her breathing as a million questions skated through her mind. She was well-aware that the symptoms she was now experiencing – dizziness and light-headedness – were from the adrenalin rush peaking in her system. She knew they would stop as soon as it abated. What she was not sure about was how she could ever reconcile the things she had just seen. What had she seen? What was that thing in her house? How had the detective survive? And where was he now?

Chapter 16

David

David flew down the stairs and out the front door. He reached the road and glanced in both directions, but the leather-clad fiend was nowhere to be seen. Somehow, the Bloodborn vampire had entered the house completely undetected. Considering he would have sensed David's presence, it was either a very bold move or a very desperate one.

Under the cover of night, David took off towards the Bloodborn's scent, tracking the miasma of rotting flesh to the end of the street where it seemed to dissipate like smoke. He stood on the corner of the road. Raked his hand through his hair. Scanned his surroundings. No movements, no sound. Nothing.

Glancing down at his bloodied shirt, he remembered the doctor's face, pale and shocked. Was she hurt? What had she seen exactly? How much of it could he reasonably explain, and would she believe him anyway? What if the vampire wasn't alone? What if others were at the house? He sped back up the street.

The front door was wide open, and he entered cautiously, closing it behind him. A sniff of the air confirmed it was just the doctor there now, and he felt relief wash over him as he heard her footsteps in the kitchen. Opening the kitchen door, he found her, pacing the floor, holding a bottle of whisky in one hand and an empty glass in the other. Her blonde hair was wild and half tucked into the collar of a long cardigan. Her feet were bare on the cold, tiled floor. He didn't need to listen for her heartbeat or smell her adrenalin to know she was spiralling with fear.

'David Sorrow,' she said, laughing. 'Did anyone ever tell you your name is sad? If it even is your name?' Her laugh sounded strange, hysterical.

'I've come down here to grab a drink,' she said, brandishing the bottle at him. 'I needed a bit of a nightcap. Something to calm my nerves. I know, I know. Alcohol is not a good self-soothing mechanism. But sometimes it helps, don't you think?'

She raised her eyebrows in David's direction as if expecting a challenge and then took a swig directly from the bottle.

'Dr Thornton—' David started.

'No!' Her voice cracked. 'Don't call me that. Today, or yesterday, I don't know what time it is now, you drove me home from hospital. You stayed on my couch. And you just fought off someone . . . something . . . from my house. I think we can be on first-name terms now.'

David nodded. He dared not make any sudden movements or disagree with her. The shift to first names seemed to make sense anyway. Dr Thornton, the rational, methodical scientist was gone. Esther, the vulnerable, scared woman, was clearly on the edge, for which he was at least partially responsible. He had dealt with quite a few unhinged people in his time as a police officer – cliff jumpers, mentally unwell, drug addicts. She had the same wild, roving eyes. His heart hurt when he looked at her.

'What exactly was that thing I saw? Because it was dark at first, and I was half asleep, and I do have a slight concussion of course, but it seemed like . . . that man was *not human*. He moved so fast, and he was strong, and he had . . . his teeth, I mean they looked like . . . like . . .' Unwilling to say the word, she kept pacing and took another swig from the bottle.

'He stabbed you with a . . . a long knife. He threw you against the wall. And you aren't that small, or light.' She poked a finger at his chest through the ripped shirt, the blood now drying into the fabric. Frowning, she backed away again, almost tripping over her own feet.

'*Did* he stab you? Is that what happened? Am I even awake?' Her face was lined with confusion.

David slowly raised his hands in a gesture of surrender as he tried to remember techniques from his training, to defuse the situation, calm her down.

'I assure you, you are wide awake. Why don't I make you some more tea, and we can sit in the lounge room and I'll explain everything?'

The doctor shook her head fiercely and backed away. 'I

don't want to sit with you. I don't want to be anywhere near you. Because you . . . you . . . what are you?'

She stopped pacing and stood in the middle of the kitchen staring at him, her arms dropping to her sides, the bottle dangling from her slack hand.

David saw it slip through her fingertips before she even registered that she was losing her grip. It hit the floor at an angle, pieces scattering across the hard tiles. Her foot, already in motion, moved forwards, not even realising what she had done.

In an instant, he was faced with almost the same choice that had been before him the night he came across her as the little girl, trapped inside her parents' ruined vehicle. He could either let her step forwards and shred her feet on the glass, or reveal who he was, lay it bare for her to see. He had failed to protect her then, decades ago, because he thought he had to hide what he was to protect everyone else. But twenty-five years of living with that choice had convinced him it was the wrong one. Glass shards crunched under his shoes as he lunged towards her, too quickly for her to see. In one fluid movement, he swept her safely into his arms and placed her carefully on the kitchen bench. She blinked rapidly, her breaths shallow as she frowned at him.

'Esther,' he said softly, trying out her first name as she had told him to. She sat mutely on the bench, unmoving.

He placed a hand gently on her elbow. She suddenly flinched and wrenched her arm free, scooting backwards. He tried not to see the look of horror on her face, the fear that came with her reaction to the truth of his existence.

'I won't hurt you,' he said, taking a step back. 'I would never hurt you.'

She levelled her gaze at him and opened her mouth to speak. It took a few tries for her words to make it out.

'What are you?' She finally managed.

David sighed in response.

What am I?

He felt like he was still answering that question for himself, even after almost one hundred and fifty years. And he certainly didn't have much practice explaining it to anyone else.

'He's a vampire,' came a soft, heavily accented voice, 'and so am I.'

Chapter 17

Essie

I'm dreaming. I must be dreaming. There's no such thing as vampires.

Essie repeated this to herself as she stared at the two men standing in her kitchen. She knew about vampires, of course. Everyone did. They were blood drinking villains or sparkly, romantic heroes. They existed in books and movies.

David Sorrow hadn't tried to suck her blood, and he didn't seem to sparkle in the daylight. He was a softly spoken policeman who wore three-piece suits.

Essie was a scientist. Science had taught her to measure, classify, and predict. Propositions are rational if they are scientifically or empirically verifiable. The bastions of logic and proof were her protection.

If vampires existed, then they would have been measured and classified. Their existence was only rational if it could be categorised and documented.

And yet she was struggling for any rational explanation

of what she had just seen. It could have been a trick of the light. Or perhaps her head injury was worse than the doctors diagnosed? There had to be a logical explanation of all this.

The detective's voice broke into her reverie. 'Esther,' he said.

Her gaze snapped to him. 'Essie,' she said reflexively. 'Just Essie.'

David helped her down from the bench and set her on the kitchen floor. The glass bottle she had dropped had been cleared away. The shorter man with slightly grey, curly hair and a dark beard moved out of their way as David took her by the elbow and guided her into an armchair in the lounge room. She moved with him as if she were a marionette, strung up to wooden sticks. He disappeared and returned in what seemed only a moment, handing her a glass of water. She took a few gulps and wiped her lips.

David sat down opposite her, as the other man appeared soundlessly behind him. 'Listen to me, Essie. This is important,' David said.

She tried to focus her eyes on him. She felt the same as when she was coming around from one of the general anaesthetics when she was a kid. Heavy limbs. Groggy mind. *Why do I feel like this?*

'Vampires aren't real,' she blurted out, her hand beginning to tremble, water splashing everywhere.

David leant forwards and gently cupped his large hands around hers, steadying the wobbling glass.

'This is a lot to take in, especially given the events

tonight. I know you've had a shock. But you need to listen to me.'

Her body was tense. She felt frozen in the moment. But something inside her – instinct? – told her that if she could just home in on David's words, they would anchor her and lead her back from the edge. It was a crazy thought to think. She didn't even believe in instinct. She didn't believe in anything that wasn't tangible and provable. But right in that moment, it was the only option she had. She looked into his eyes and sat up straight.

'Vampires are real,' he said steadily. 'Rafael and I are vampires. We have walked this earth for over a century, several centuries in his case.'

Essie shook her head. David was in his mid to late thirties at most. The grey-haired man, Rafael, was definitely older, but not over one hundred years old. No one could be that old.

'No. That's not possible.'

Rafael stepped forwards and whispered something into David's ear, but David raised his hand to silence him.

'Everything I am saying is the truth. How else do you explain what you have seen with your own eyes tonight?'

Essie traced back over the events of the evening again in her mind. The fight upstairs, the other man who moved with such strength and speed. David, standing before her now, without so much as a mark except for his bloodied shirt. The man had thrown him against the wall with enough force his bones should have splintered like kindling. He stabbed him too. Yet, here he was, completely fine.

'Who was that other man in my house tonight?'

'We don't know yet.'

'Was he a . . .' She couldn't bring herself to use the word.

'Yes. I chased him out into the street, but he got away.'

'But if he was one of you, a *vampire*, why did he attack you?'

David glanced over his shoulder at Rafael, as if seeking permission. He stood motionless.

'You may as well tell her the rest, *Dado*.'

David nodded and turned back to Essie.

'Rafael and I are Amaranthine vampires, or half-vampires. We exist in hereditary pairs. One makes the other, and the two exist as the elder and the younger until the elder passes away. Then, and only then, the younger may make a new vampire. But there are others. They are Bloodborn vampires. They are not restricted to living in pairs like us. They can make other vampires at will. The vampire who was here tonight is one of them.'

Essie took another sip of water and felt her mind begin to clear, like slivers of sunlight breaking through on a foggy morning. If what David said was true, it didn't mean there wasn't a scientific explanation for it. It just meant it hadn't been discovered yet. Though she wasn't a biologist, she couldn't deny her curiosity was piqued. Science had been seeking the secrets of long life since time immemorial. Maybe someone, somewhere, had actually figured it out.

'Bloodborns,' she repeated slowly, trying out the phrase, as if saying it might make it more believable.

David stood and raked his hand through his hair, causing it to stand out at slightly odd angles.

'It's a long story. The Bloodborns were here first, or so the story goes. Made by an ancient god, to be his own personal army. They went to war against the humans, to subdue them as a slave race. But a small group of humans managed to steal the god's blood and use it to make the Amaranthine, hybrid human-vampires, to prevent the Bloodborns from succeeding.'

Essie suppressed a laugh of disbelief.

'Look, vampires are one thing. I might be able to believe there's some scientific explanation for the two of you. But seriously, ancient gods, wars?'

David nodded.

'I can understand your scepticism, but it's what we know of our origins. More importantly, I think that vampire who was here tonight is somehow connected to your bike accident, but I'm not so sure it was an accident.'

She pushed her glasses up her nose and slumped back into the armchair. Rafael was watching her intently. She could feel his eyes on her. He was so still though, like a mime artist in a street show.

'You think that man, that vampire, is who I ran into in the laneway?'

David paced in a little circle. He was the opposite of Rafael, all motion and energy and unsettled. 'Yes. But he obviously didn't get what he wanted because he came back tonight to finish the job.'

Essie touched her hand to her head. It was still tender. Her back was aching as well. She stood up and wrapped her arms around herself. A sudden movement in her peripheral vision made her whip her head around. Rafael now stood beside her, and she started back in shock.

'Raf,' David scolded him, clearly annoyed. 'Slow movements. She's had enough excitement for one night.'

Rafael inclined his head. 'Apologies, Dr Thornton. Just a little test, if you will.'

Essie's brow creased, and she put her hands on her hips.

'A test? Of what exactly?'

'Of how surprising you find it when a vampire suddenly appears beside you,' he smiled sardonically.

Essie squared her shoulders and stepped towards him, anger burning through her.

'Why are you testing *me*? A man was in my house tonight, and I think he would have killed me if David wasn't here.'

'Exactly,' Rafael said, holding his ground. 'Why was that man here? Why were you attacked in the laneway? If you aren't working with them, you must have something they want.'

She remembered the missing notebook with a pang, and a cold shiver snaked down her back. Was it possible these evil vampires, the Bloodborns, had taken it? Why would they do that? It was meaningless to anyone else, especially without the other half.

Up close to him, she noticed Rafael's eyes had changed colour from a bland brown to a burnt orange, like a sunset. The change made his whole face take on a different hue, pale and ethereal.

'Rafael,' David warned, inserting himself between them. 'For the last time, she is not working with the Bloodborns!'

'Vampires, Bloodborns, Ama—' Essie broke off, trying to remember the fancy word David had used.

'Amaranthine,' he finished for her. 'It means ageless.'

'This is completely nuts!' She shook her head, backing away. 'Insane.'

'I understand it must seem that way,' David conceded. 'But it's all true.'

Essie glanced back and forth between him and Rafael. Even though she didn't fully understand what she had seen, she felt like her head was finally clear again. The cobwebs were being fully blown out. Maybe David's and Rafael's existence could be rationalised? There were lots of things people in the past didn't understand or had attributed to magic that science had eventually explained. She thought she could probably figure them out. She just needed some time and space to think. And she definitely didn't need them in her house while she was trying to do it.

'I want you both to leave. Now.'

'Essie,' David said, taking a step towards her.

She picked up her phone from the coffee table and held down the power button to switch it on.

'If you don't leave, I'm going to call the police.' She hesitated, remembering David's job. 'I mean the other police, that aren't you,' she said, waving the phone at him.

David opened his mouth to respond to her when a sharp, jangling noise rang out. It took Essie a moment to recognise it. She'd had her phone switched off or turned to silent for so long she forgot that it was her ringtone. She slid the call accept button reflexively.

'Hello,' she mumbled, shouldering the handset against her ear, her eyes fixed on the two men in her lounge room.

'Dr Thornton?' asked a quiet voice on the other end of the line.

'Yes,' she responded impatiently. The memory of the barrage of prank calls and messages from the last few days flooded over her, and she cursed herself for answering.

'I'm calling from the Central West Hospital. You're listed as Cecil Armstrong's next of kin.'

Cecil? What? Her stomach flipped.

'What's happened? Is he all right?' David caught her eye, his face concerned.

'No, he's not well. He had a stroke late last night. I've been trying to call you and left a few messages. The ambulance bought him in a while ago. You should come to the hospital as soon as you can.'

Her stomach tightened, and she struggled to order her thoughts.

'I'll come straight away.' She hung up the phone and glanced down at her now two-day old outfit.

'I have to go to the hospital,' she said, moving towards the staircase.

'What's wrong?' He asked, catching her elbow as she tried to push past him.

'It's my friend, Cecil, he was taken to the hospital in an ambulance last night. He's had a stroke.' Hot tears stung at her eyes.

'I'll drive you,' he said, without hesitation. She noticed Rafael throw him a meaningful look, but he didn't say anything.

Turning her gaze back to David, she could see his pupils up close. Finally, it dawned on her what was different about his eyes. They were the same as Rafael's. They *had* actually changed colour. Instead of the soft blue she had noticed in the daylight, they were now a darker shade, almost the colour of midnight. Fascinating. There was likely a scientific explanation for the eye colours. Some genetic aberration, or a heat reaction. The other things about him were harder to explain. She didn't really want to accept more help from the detective, or vampire, or vampire-detective, whatever his real identity might be. Just minutes ago, she had been trying to throw him out of her house. But Cecil needed her, now. And it was still the early hours of the morning. She couldn't ride her bike in her current state and the buses wouldn't run for a few hours. She could order a taxi, but that would take a while.

'Okay. But I need to get changed,' she said, disengaging her arm from his grip and heading up the staircase.

Chapter 18

David

D avid buttoned his suit jacket over his ruined shirt while he waited for Essie to change. Fortunately, the jacket hid the worst of the damage. Essie came back down the stairs two at a time. She had changed into jeans and an over-sized green shirt. The scent hit him hard. Her shirt reeked of the same woody smell he had first detected in Anna's apartment and then in Essie's room. He swallowed and exchanged a glance with Rafael, shaking his head discreetly. Now hardly seemed the time to tell her a murderer had been in her bedroom and touched her clothes. Essie grabbed a grey coat from the stand in the entryway, slinging it around her shoulders as she marched towards the front door.

'I will wait here. Our Bloodborn friend might return,' Rafael said.

Essie swung around and scowled at him before turning on her heels.

'Fine,' Essie said over her shoulder as she opened the front door.

ESSIE STARED out the window of the passenger seat as David's car sped down the freeway, her profile silhouetted by the pre-dawn light. He was finding it hard to read her. Though initially she had reacted slightly hysterically, which was understandable, now she seemed to be handling the night's events quite calmly. Her heart rate was normal, and she smelled normal, except for the shirt.

'How long have you been a . . . vampire?' She asked softly. His heart clenched. He knew she would have questions. But there were some he wasn't sure how to answer. He kept his eyes on the road as he spoke.

'Nearly one hundred and forty years.'

'How old were you when . . .'

'Thirty-six.'

She was silent for a moment.

'So, you're telling me you were born in the 1880s?'

'1882,' he said, changing his grip on the steering wheel.

'I've seen the movies. You sleep in a coffin, you aren't supposed to walk in the daylight, you need to be invited into someone's house, you shouldn't drink tea . . .'

'Myths,' he said flatly.

'So, tea is all you drink?' she asked pointedly.

He pulled the car into a visitor parking spot at the hospital and went to the passenger side to open the door for her. He didn't know how to give her a purely factual response on that question. But she was already climbing out of her seat, her face hard with a grim expression as she walked off. David pressed the lock button on his key and ran after her as she hurried through the sliding doors of the emergency department.

'I'm here for Cecil Armstrong,' she said breathlessly to the nurse at the front desk. 'He was brought in earlier with a stroke.'

The nurse squinted at the computer screen in front of her and clicked the mouse a few times. 'The doctor is still assessing him. Take a seat over there and someone will call you when you can go through.' She indicated a low bench seat to the right of the nurses' station.

Essie looked ready to protest the woman's instructions, then turned away and sat down. David sank down beside her, careful not to sit too close, nor too far away. As a rule, he didn't like being in hospitals. Too much life, too many hearts beating erratically, the full gamut of human experience, birth to death, all wrapped up in one building. But he found he wasn't thinking about that tonight. His attention was preoccupied by the woman next to him. Her heart was racing, and her blood took on the now-familiar tang it had when she was upset.

'Would you like me to come in with you?' he offered.

She paused for a moment before looking up at him.

'No,' she answered, staring straight ahead and pulling the folds of her coat together.

'Of course,' David said, smiling tightly. He instinctively began to prepare himself for her rejection. After all, he had turned the world as she knew it upside down tonight. He remembered how he had felt when Rafael first showed him the truth. It was frightening, overwhelming, and caused him to question everything. It was a wild cocktail of emotions.

Essie turned to him suddenly and put her hand on his arm.

'Just wait out here, but don't do anything *weird,*' she said, raising her eyebrows and glancing about furtively. Across from them, a harassed-looking woman sat bouncing a little girl on her knee. A bearded man sat next to them, holding a fat bandage over his thumb. Neither of them looked up as she spoke.

David leaned in closer to her.

'I wouldn't dream of it.'

Essie pushed her glasses up her nose and wrapped a lock of hair behind her ear. A middle-aged man in a white lab coat with a manila folder tucked under his arm came towards them.

'Dr Thornton, is it?'

'Yes,' Essie said.

'I'm Tim Cain, the emergency registrar. Mr Armstrong has you listed as his next of kin.' He sat down on the other side of Essie as she lowered herself back onto the bench.

'He has no family here,' Essie responded quietly. 'His wife, Sarah, died a few years ago.'

Dr Cain nodded and flipped open the manila folder. He had a kind face, but also the cool air of a professional going through the motions of his daily routine. He was practically bald and the top of his head was shiny under the harsh hospital lighting. He took a pen from his breast pocket and tapped it absently on the file, before making some quick notes.

'He's eighty-four years old. Generally in good health, apart from his hip?'

'Arthritis,' Essie confirmed. 'Last time I saw him, he seemed fine. He said he'd had a cold the week before, but he was getting better.'

The doctor flipped a page in the folder and read the notes.

'He saw his GP last Thursday, who recommended he come to the emergency department to get checked out. We have no record of him coming in though. His neighbour noticed him collapsed in the back courtyard last night. She called the ambulance.'

Essie nodded in a composed way, but David saw her hands were shaking as she fidgeted non-stop with the buttons on her coat.

'He was probably out there watching for the pardalotes. There's this pair of pardalotes nesting in his retaining wall. They're these tiny, tiny birds – almost like butterflies . . .' Her voice trailed off, and she swiped a tear from her cheek.

'He'll be okay, though. Won't he?' she asked.

The doctor inclined his head in a non-committal way. David had seen that look on doctors' faces a hundred times in the field. The war in Skhodra, both the World Wars. It was always the same. The truth was, they didn't know. Any power they seemed to have over life and death was an illusion.

'It's too soon to say. We don't know how long he was

unconscious, which complicates the treatment options. We're monitoring him. Is there anyone else you should call?'

'I can try his sister. She lives in the Greek Islands.'

The doctor nodded and replaced his pen in his breast pocket as he closed the folder. 'I think that would be a good idea. I can take you through to see him now for a short visit. He's on a ventilator to help him breath, and he's not conscious.'

'Okay,' Essie agreed, standing to follow the doctor.

Dr Cain swiped his hospital security pass. David watched as Essie disappeared through the doors. He sat back on the long bench and laced his hands behind his head, letting out a sigh. The baby began to fuss, and the woman bounced it rhythmically on her knee, trying to soothe its cries. He wished there was more he could do for Essie. It didn't feel right letting her go in alone. His phone buzzed with a message from Morton. He ignored it and put the phone back in his pocket.

Chapter 19

Essie

The hospital smell hit Essie fiercely again. Then there was the familiar ticking and beeping of machines and pumps. After weeks spent on a ward when she was a child, followed by a series of skin graft operations, rehab and physio, Essie had avoided going anywhere near a hospital for twenty years. Yet here she was, for the second time in as many days. She had to psyche herself up so much to enter the building that she practically ran through the emergency department doors before she lost her nerve.

Dr Cain led her along a corridor and into a room with several beds separated by blue plastic curtains, patients lined up like dominoes. The doctor pushed a curtain to one side, revealing another small cubicle that had the luxury of actual walls on two sides because it was at the end of the row. It was decorated on one wall with a drab, nondescript landscape print and on the other, a jarringly bright photograph of balloons, all in primary colours. She recognised the ineffective attempt to distract people from a confronting environment.

The Cecil who lay on the thin hospital bed was not her Cecil at all. His skin had a greyish hue. His closed eyes were sunken in the sockets and his mouth lay slack and open, a ventilation tube taped securely to his papery cheek. His head was almost prone on the bed, propped up only by one thin, white pillow. A strand of his thinning grey hair lay loosely across his forehead. She wanted to reach out and brush it from his face. He always kept his hair so neatly. He would have hated it.

Should she have seen this coming? Was there some sign at dinner she missed? She had probably been too caught up in her own selfish concerns to notice anything was wrong.

'We've made him comfortable,' Dr Cain said.

Essie pushed the visitor's chair closer to the bedside. 'Can I touch him?'

'Yes, by all means,' the doctor said. She brushed the hair off Cecil's forehead and smoothed it neatly to the side. Perching on the edge of the chair, she took his hand in both of hers. His lined skin still seemed smooth next to the mottled redness of her burn-scarred hand. But his coldness, against the warmth of her skin, shocked her.

'I'm just going to check on another patient and see if Mr Armstrong's CT scan has come back,' Dr Cain murmured, pulling the plastic curtain partially closed as he left.

Essie's stomach twisted and the tears that she had

been fighting since she first received the phone call now flowed freely down her face.

'Cecil, you have to wake up,' she said, sniffing. 'I need you to wake up. What about the faculty social events? Who will talk to me if you're not there? And what about our dinners? What will happen if we can't have dinner anymore?'

Cecil lay there, resolutely silent. The sound of the ventilator providing his breaths was so mechanical. The heart monitor beeped rhythmically. Essie wished she could shut the noise out.

'The worst thing is, I never got to tell you . . .' She broke off, sobbing. Lowering her forehead to his hand, she lay her cheek against his palm. 'I never got to tell you how important you are to me. Do you know how glad I am that my tyre went flat that day we met?'

She didn't believe in God. He was in the same category as vampires had been. He wasn't tangible or measurable. But in that moment, she found herself closing her eyes and praying. She prayed he would wake up. Prayed that he would turn his kind eyes on her.

A slight breeze made the plastic curtain tremble and Essie sensed a movement behind her. She sat up, wiping vainly at her cheeks with the sleeve of her coat.

'Here,' David said quietly, passing her his handkerchief over her shoulder.

She turned and took the square of fabric from him, shaking it out.

'I thought I said to wait outside.'

'You did,' David said. 'But I have observed over the

years that sometimes, what people say and what they mean are different things.' He carefully moved Cecil's folded clothing from the other visitor's chair and placed it on the shelf beside the bed. The chair legs scraped across the linoleum floor as he moved it a little closer to Essie and sat down.

'How did you even get in here? The doors are swipe access,' Essie sniffed, blotting her eyes and nose with the handkerchief.

David merely raised his eyebrows. 'Oh,' Essie fumbled. 'So, you can mind control people, I suppose?'

'No,' David grinned. 'Another myth. But I am fast. I don't have to be seen if I don't wish to be.'

Essie looked at him under the harsh hospital lighting. How could she not have realised what he was before tonight? The answer came to her like a knife stabbing her heart.

Just like how you missed the signs of Cecil's stroke. Always too caught up in your own problems to notice what is going on around you.

In hindsight, a collection of tiny tells clicked into place in her mind. David's three-piece suits, the formal handwriting, his mannerisms. They were of a different time. All those seemed like obvious clues now.

But it was his physical appearance that struck her at that moment. She noticed his eyes again. They had returned to cerulean blue. That seemed their most usual colour. His skin was pale, but not like Cecil's. It had a translucent quality like skimmed milk, yet it seemed stony and hard at the same time, reminding her of alabaster. And though he was tall and his long arms seemed gangly, she now knew what he was capable of and sensed a restraint in the way he held himself. It was as if he were constantly working hard to hold back a tidal wave of energy. She hesitated to use the word, but the only way to describe him was *otherworldly*.

The cubicle's plastic curtain was noisily swept aside, and Essie turned her head as Dr Cain appeared. 'I have some test results,' he said, taking Cecil's clipboard chart from the end of the bed and sitting in the chair where David had been a moment before.

'It's not good news. The CT scan shows that Mr Armstrong was probably out for some time before the neighbours found him. There's been extensive bleeding on his brain.' Dr Cain paused. Waited. A deep ache lodged in Essie's heart and she felt she might suffocate.

'In these situations, it's difficult to give a prognosis with any certainty, but his age is not in his favour. If he were to survive without breathing support, he would need extensive rehabilitation and, even then, his quality of life would likely be quite compromised.'

She nodded and pursed her lips together tightly, worried if she spoke, she would cry again.

Don't say it.

Her gaze drifted to the ceiling.

Don't say there's nothing we can do.

Dr Cain flicked over a page on his clipboard and held it between two fingers, cross-referencing something with the previous page. 'Dr Thornton, because you are listed as Mr Armstrong's next of kin . . .'

'Cecil!' she snapped. 'His name is Cecil.'

'You are Cecil's next of kin,' the doctor said patiently. 'So you have some say in what we do from here.'

'You have to keep trying. You must be able to give him something to stop the bleeding, reduce the swelling. Anything. I'll try calling his sister now.'

The doctor nodded slowly and closed the clipboard.

'All right,' he agreed. 'You'll need to go out into the waiting room to make the call. We don't allow mobile phone use in here.'

'Fine,' Essie said, rising from her chair. She glanced back at Cecil briefly and made her way back down the corridor, her vision blurring with unshed tears pooling in her eyes.

She wasn't entirely sure how she made it back to the bench seat, where David sat waiting, as if he had never left it. Essie stood in front of him and pushed her fogged up glasses onto the top of her head. She wiped her eyes with the handkerchief again and put it in her pocket.

'I need to call Cecil's sister, Mary,' she said, rummaging for the mobile phone in her pocket. She squeezed the power button and tapped at the blank screen. No response. The battery had died.

'Do you want me to call? I've had some experience at delivering this type of news.'

Essie shook her head. 'I should do it. But I don't know the number.' She showed him her dead screen. 'She lives in the Greek Islands.'

David took out his phone. 'Same surname?'

'No. She got married to a Greek man. I think her full

name is Marjorie, Marjorie Katsaros,' she said, slumping down on the seat beside him. He spoke to someone on the other end of the phone, asking for international dialling details.

'Which island?' he whispered, holding the phone slightly away from his ear.

'Corfu.'

David nodded and turned away as he spoke into the phone again.

Thank goodness David was with the police. A few seconds later, he passed her the handset with Mary on the other end. Essie relayed all the information Dr Cain had given her. Mary was understandably upset, but not surprised. It sounded like she had been expecting the call.

'I'll be on the first flight I can get,' she said, her voice slightly choked.

'Okay,' Essie agreed, sniffing again as she pressed the used handkerchief to her nose. 'What should I do . . . what should I tell the doctors . . .'

'Cecil speaks so highly of you. I know he made you his next of kin, in legal things. You do whatever you think is the right thing to do, dear.' Mary had the same turn of phrase and lilt to her voice as Cecil. It was comforting.

'All right,' Essie promised. 'You have my number. Just call me when you get here.' Mary promised she would, and Essie hung up the call.

'Thanks,' she said, handing the phone back to David.

'You did well,' he smiled.

Dr Cain appeared in the waiting room.

'I just spoke to his sister. She's coming as soon as she can.'

'Good,' the doctor said. 'Do you want to come and sit with him again?'

Essie turned to leave before spinning on her heels to face David.

'Would you come with me? Please?'

He held her gaze for a moment. 'Of course.'

The pair sat down by Cecil's bed in silence, watching the rhythmic rise and fall of his chest. Essie squeezed her eyes closed for a moment, hoping that when she opened them again, she might wake up and find it was all a nightmare. How could this be happening? How could any of the things that happened in the last forty-eight hours be real?

The heart monitor began beeping erratically, and Essie's lids flicked open as a nurse rushed into the room. She hit a red button over Cecil's bed and Dr Cain appeared, accompanied by another nurse with a ponytail and a stethoscope draped around her neck.

'He's arresting,' Dr Cain said, sweeping Essie and David back from the bed. She leaned into David's side and felt his hand grasp hers.

The nurse removed the respirator from Cecil's tube and began pumping oxygen manually via a bag. The heart monitor flatlined in a long, drawn-out monotone. Dr Cain held the defibrillator pads over Cecil's chest. He leaned forwards and the nurse stopped pumping the bag and stood back. Dr Cain shocked Cecil with the pads once, and all eyes in the room went to the heart monitor. It continued to flatline.

Essie clapped her hand to her mouth as the air left her lungs. She struggled to get breathe in again, as if it were her lying on the hospital bed, fighting for her life. 'No, no,' she mouthed.

Dr Cain charged the defibrillator again while the nurse with the ponytail listened to Cecil's chest with the stethoscope. The doctor called for everyone to clear and she stepped back as he leaned forwards and shocked Cecil again. Cecil's chest rose and fell with the electric current, but the monitor continued to show no response. The nurse did not resume manually pumping the air as she looked to Dr Cain for her queue. He shook his head slightly.

'I don't think we will be able to get him back, Dr Thornton,' he said gently. Essie shook her head as tears poured down her face. She dropped David's hand and lunged forwards. Shoving the nurse out of her way, she grabbed Cecil's hand and held it to her cheek again, rubbing it gently.

'Cecil,' she whispered, 'Cecil, please wake up.'

You have to wake up, Cecil. Moffatt still needs you to take care of him. I still need you to take care of me!

She wasn't sure how long she stood there, cradling his hand against her face, the sobs racking her body like the electrical current they had used to try to revive him. At some point, David took her by the shoulders and pulled her back from the edge of the bed. He guided her into the chair and sat down beside her. When she looked up, the nurses and doctors had left. They covered Cecil's chest with a sheet. All the medical tape was gone from his face. He still didn't look like himself, but he looked more peaceful.

A heaviness descended on her, like a medicine ball resting on her chest. She felt numb under its weight. She could hear the air coming in and leaving her body, but it was like breathing underwater. After a while, she felt the gentle pressure of David's hand on her shoulder.

'Essie, we should go,' he said. 'They need to prepare Cecil's body.'

He lowered his voice and leaned in.

'And I am concerned about us being here, out in the open.'

Essie dragged her eyes away from Cecil and nodded at him. How could she push the pallor of grief away and focus on the other pressing problems in her life right now? It was too much. Too much. But David was also right. She couldn't sit there in the emergency department forever. When he reached for her hand, she let him lead her away from the curtained cubicle.

Chapter 20

David

After they sorted out the administrative affairs at the hospital, Essie called Mary from the car as they drove to David's flat. He heard Mary sob quietly before saying she would take care of all the funeral arrangements.

'I have his neighbour's number. I'll call and see if they can feed Moffatt for now,' Mary said.

'Okay. I'll talk to you again when you arrive.'

'Thank you, Essie. Thank you for everything.'

Meanwhile, David had spoken to Rafael but ignored another missed phone call. His pocket buzzed anew with unchecked messages. Morton was probably getting worried. But there wasn't time for that yet.

Essie followed him mutely inside his apartment and he settled her on the lounge with a cup of tea. He wished he had something more to offer her than the slightly out-of-date shortbreads he had purchased for a work event a while ago and forgotten about.

When did she last eat?

Humans needed to eat, especially if they'd been through something traumatic.

'I need to change my shirt,' he said, leaving her in the lounge room. He also took the opportunity to consume his own liquid nourishment. Out of her sight.

When he returned, buttoning his clean shirt, she was still wearing her coat, her eyes puffy and red-rimmed. The biscuits sat on a plate in her lap, untouched.

'Rafael and I decided it was safer to bring you here. We don't think they know this place.' He tucked in the shirt and pulled his vest back on over it. She made no response.

He stood and watched her for a moment. Having someone in his flat besides Rafael was strange. His lifestyle didn't lend itself to entertaining guests.

Her scent filled the room, a heady mix of the human spruce smell from Anna's flat, with underlying notes that were distinctly Essie – sweet cloves and soap. It was very distracting.

Though David hadn't known Cecil, watching Essie's grief was still difficult. Even at a distance, loss was hard, and it hurt. The accumulation of loss, over hundreds of years, was enough to drive anyone insane. The Bloodborns, with their lack of humanity, were not given to that type of madness. But Rafael had seen it happen to Amaranthine. His friend's longstanding advice rang in his ears again. Don't get involved, don't get close.

But I am involved. It's too late.

It was as though there was some unseen force pulling him towards Essie. In over a century as a vampire, he had never met the same human twice. Of course, he and Rafael

145

took steps to prevent it. While it wasn't beyond the realm of possibility he should meet Essie again, in a city of over a million people, in a different time and place, it seemed against the odds. And now she was being hunted by a Bloodborn. Was it merely coincidence that led him back to the little girl he had not saved? He wasn't sure if he believed in fate or destiny, but he couldn't help feeling that somehow, he was being given a second chance.

'I am sorry for your loss,' he said quietly. 'How did you meet Cecil, if I may ask?'

A sad smile crossed her face.

'I got a flat tyre on my bike one day near work. I was on the side of the road changing it when he drove up and offered to help. I didn't need his help. I've changed lots of flat tyres. I've never had a drivers' licence. I was in a car accident when I was little.'

'Yes,' David said, clearing his throat. 'I read about that in your father's missing persons' file.'

Essie nodded. 'Oh. Well, there was something about the way Cecil patiently insisted on helping. Normally I'd find it annoying, but with him, it was different. We got talking about science. Looking back, I think he was lonely too. His wife died a few years ago.'

She dropped her gaze.

'But it was foolish for me to get close to him. He was already old when we met. This was bound to happen.'

David frowned and tilted his head. 'I disagree. It is precisely for that reason that you are fortunate to have known him.'

'What do you mean?'

'A chance meeting over a flat tyre brought two people together and you became friends. No matter how short-lived. True friendship is a rare and wonderful thing.'

Essie stared down into her teacup. 'If it's so wonderful, then why does it hurt so much? I think it's better to be alone than to feel like this.'

David sat down beside her and fished out a clean handkerchief from his pocket. She took it from him with a short laugh and blew her nose.

'Losing people we love hurts, but so does loneliness. All of us long for connection, to be known, to be really seen by another person. And all of us experience pain when that connection is broken. It doesn't mean it wasn't worth it. Actually, the opposite is true. The pain reminds us how much we loved and were loved.'

Essie raised her tear-stained face to his and stared at him for a long moment. He couldn't tell if she understood what he was trying to say, or if she was ready to punch him. The sharp angles of her face softened and she frowned.

'Are you really one hundred and forty years old?'

'One hundred and thirty-nine. My birthday isn't until September,' he smiled, and she did too. The tension melted from his muscles.

She shoved half a shortbread into her mouth and stood up, crumbs tumbling onto his floor. He sensed a shift in her mood.

'Okay,' she said, swallowing. 'I'm not saying I believe everything you told me, especially the stuff about the gods and monsters. But let's say I believe you and Rafael are who you say you are – *what* you say you are.'

David's heart lightened. He could almost see the cogs ticking over in her brain as she catalogued all the information she had so far. She may not have fully accepted the truth, but she was trying.

'I have some questions.'

He eased back into the lounge, bracing himself. She began pacing in a little circle as she spoke.

'David Sorrow isn't your real name, is it?'

He inclined his head in part answer.

'David is my Christian name. But I was born David Maric. I've changed my surname many times over the decades.'

'But Rafael, he called you something else – *Dado*?'

She trailed off. He smiled. She didn't miss much. Even with everything she had been through, with the shock and horror of it all, she had been paying attention.

'*Dado*. It's Croatian. It's the equivalent of 'Dave' in English. A nickname.'

'So you're from Croatia originally? But you don't have an accent. How long have you lived in Australia?'

'Not long, relatively speaking. But I've had over one hundred years to practice my English, as well as some other languages,' he said.

Essie stood, shrugged off her coat and tossed it over the back of the couch.

'One hundred and forty years. Wow,' she shook her head.

'Raf is older. I'm not exactly sure how much older.' He'd

never told David either his human age or how long he had been Amaranthine, although he mentioned being at Henry VIII's court once.

'But Rafael still has an accent . . . an Italian accent? Did he live in Italy for a long time?'

'Yes. He was born in Italy. But that's not why he has an accent. I mentioned we are a hereditary pair. It's a failsafe that the humans built in when they created the Amaranthine to ensure that we could never become truly immortal or too numerous. We aren't like the Bloodborns. Our creation involves sacrifice on the part of the creator.' He paused to give Essie a moment to take in the information.

'When Rafael made me, he gave up his immortality. He's still a vampire, but his body began aging again, albeit at a much slower pace than humans. We call it reverting. He is showing signs of physical deterioration, on and off, including regressing to his earliest habits at times. Language learning is seated deep in our memory. It's getting harder for Raf to easily recall all the other languages he knows. His mind is aging backwards, in a way. Eventually, he will only be able to speak Italian again.'

Essie stopped pacing and stared at him, scratched her head and blinked.

'Speaking as a scientist, what you're telling me is completely unbelievable. It's impossible.'

He nodded an acknowledgment of her observations and waited for her to continue. She squared her shoulders and locked her eyes on him.

'In the car, you didn't answer me when I asked about your diet.'

He winced. There was no way this could be a comfortable conversation. But he had to tell her. She needed to know.

'Blood is life for all, I'm afraid, just in different ways. You have about five litres of blood circulating around your body at any given time.'

She raised an eyebrow at him.

'That's not the same thing.'

He shrugged.

'I can eat food and drink tea, but it doesn't nourish me. I need blood for that.' He glanced up at her. 'But not five litres and not every day.' He hoped she understood what that meant. That he was no threat to her. That he was different from them.

'So, you only kill to survive? Like once or twice a year, or what are we talking about?'

David shook his head emphatically.

'I don't kill humans for blood, ever. Protecting humans from the Bloodborns is the reason we exist. I can drink animal blood and there are blood banks. I have drunk from humans who were already deceased, if I had no other choice. That's a last resort though.'

Essie screwed up her nose at him. He tried not to think of all the battlefields he'd been on in France, Singapore, New Guinea – soldiers' bodies piled one on top of the other, and the burning thirst in the back of his throat that refused to be sated any other way.

'The Bloodborns are different. Blood is an addiction for

them,' he continued. 'At first, most of them can't control their bloodlust at all. It's the only thing they can think about. The slightest whiff of blood and they turn feral. They gain more self-control as they age, but they still care nothing for human life. Once they are reborn, they lose their humanity entirely. In their eyes, humans become like animals – a source of food or labour. They will drink their fill and more, unless they plan to make a new vampire.'

Essie shot him a look of disbelief.

'If there were vampires going around drinking people's blood for hundreds of years, we'd know. Humans would have worked it out by now,' she said, her hands on her hips.

'Humans used to know, used to believe things like that. But now . . . science has explained all the mysteries of the universe.' He couldn't resist smirking at her. She pursed her lips and raised her eyebrows at him in response.

'The Bloodborns' numbers have also dwindled,' he continued. 'Bloodborns are volatile and unpredictable by nature. But over the last century or so, they have begun to fight amongst themselves, sometimes cannibalising each other. They also hunt the weakest in society, those that no one will care about enough to investigate. And the Amaranthine have always been working behind the scenes, in jobs like mine, gaining access to things that allowed us to conceal what the humans should not see.'

'So, you've been covering up their crimes?' she asked, aghast.

'Only to protect humans. Most people aren't ready to understand what you have seen. They just want to go on existing in ignorance.' Essie sighed resignedly, yet the set of her eyes made him see she was not finished questioning.

'But you don't age. You still look thirty-six. People must notice.'

'Yes, eventually.' His mind went to the conversation he had overheard between Morton and Orbost. 'But we move around a lot. It's why we came to Australia.'

She shook her head, still resisting. He had to admire her thoroughness.

'But there are autopsies and the internet and social media – surely someone with a phone would have caught something on camera by now?'

David shrugged and spread his hands expansively.

'You've seen how fast we are. Even if someone did catch one of us on camera, it would be a blur, indiscernible. Or people would think it's manipulated. It's easier now days than ever to edit footage or images. We are like Big Foot or the Loch Ness Monster. We've made rich fodder for fiction writers over the centuries. There's a kernel of truth in all of it, of course, but no proof.'

Essie pressed her lips together and blinked hard. Was she finally running out of logical arguments?

'Okay. So, there was one of these other vampires – Bloodborns – in my house last night. Why?'

David grimaced. 'Not only last night, I'm afraid. He had been there before we got back from the hospital too.'

'What?' she breathed.

'I sensed it the minute I stepped through your front door. He had been there – probably in the last few days.'

'The noise I heard . . .' she said thoughtfully. 'The day

you came to interview me about Steenberger's murder, that night I kept waking up to strange noises in the house. But I just put it down to my nerves being on edge.'

He nodded. 'It could have been him. Your front door was jammed when we got home, remember? He might have damaged it breaking in. I'm sorry, but there's more.'

He leaned forwards, tenting his fingers and resting his elbows on his knees.

'Whoever caused Anna's death is somehow linked to you as well. At her flat, I identified another scent. But it wasn't Bloodborns. It was human.'

Essie's eyebrows drew together in confusion.

'Bloodborns all smell the same to me,' he explained. 'But human scents are unique, like fingerprints. The same scent from Anna's flat was in your house too, in your bedroom.'

She took a step back and hugged herself. David wanted to reassure her, but there wasn't much he could say that would help.

'So, whoever killed Anna had been in my bedroom?'

He nodded.

'You, Anna and her killer are connected. And it can't be a coincidence that the Bloodborns came after you at the same time. There has to be something that is tying this all together.'

Essie retreated to the window and turned her face away from him. He heard her heartbeat kick up a notch. *Thump-thump, thump-thump*, it sounded a loud staccato. Something was wrong. What was she still hiding?

'Essie, I've trusted you with the most important secret that I have,' he said slowly.

She drew in a deep breath. He watched her shoulders rise and fall with it.

'I'm on your side. I want to help, but there's still something you are holding back.'

She turned around, her face displaying her inner conflict with its drawn lines, eyebrows pulled together. She was clearly weighing her next words carefully.

'I think I might know how we're all connected,' she spoke softly. 'But I'm not sure where to begin.'

'Take your time. I'm not going anywhere.' David patted the seat next to him.

She fidgeted with the handkerchief as she sat down, twisting the folds of fabric, her eyes rooted to the floor.

'I think this is all about my dad. I told the police I had no idea what happened to him. But the truth is, I have a pretty good idea, and it's all my fault.'

Chapter 21

Essie

'Dad was the one who first introduced me to Issachar Zion and his theories of quantum mechanics. He bought home his biography from a second-hand store in town when I was a kid.'

Essie smiled at the memory of Gilbert handing her the battered book. He always brought her random presents, things other people thought were junk. Her mother told her he was like a bowerbird. The book had smelled funny, but Essie liked the solid feel of the hardback in her hands. The black-and-white photo of Zion on the inside fly leaf was already faded with time.

'Dad said he gave it to me because Zion reminded him of me – he was curious about the world and how things worked. He said it was an amazing gift.'

Maybe her father had been right. Curiosity had led her to the greatest discovery of her life, perhaps the greatest scientific discovery ever. But it had also led to that woman on the other end of the phone who wanted to take her discovery and pervert it to her own ends. It led to lies and deceit and doing things she never thought she was capable of doing. A knot had formed in her stomach the day of the first phone call and if she was honest, it had never really relaxed. Then her father was gone. Sitting next to the detective in his flat right now, the knot tightened further, and Essie's breaths were coming in shallow bursts. She glanced around, struggling with what to say next.

David's apartment was so sparse. No tea stains on the coffee table, no drying laundry or burnt food smell. She wasn't sure what she had expected to find in the apartment of a man who was over one hundred years old. Maybe more antiques? Valuable art? There was a nice rug on the floor that looked Persian. And there was the black leather lounge they sat on now. But there wasn't much else. No knickknacks, no photo frames. Precision and order. It smelled like him, unsurprisingly. A hint of black coffee and worn leather, like an old pair of gloves. Her eyes fell on him. He was watching her, waiting. She inhaled again.

'He tried so hard after my mum . . . after the car accident. It was just the two of us then. And I let him down,' she sniffed. The tears started again. She was almost getting used to it, the unveiled show of emotion. Holding it back took more energy than she could muster now. The skin on her hand ached and tingled and she massaged it restlessly.

David leaned towards her and took both her hands in his. He felt shockingly warm for someone who was apparently dead. Or at least not wholly alive.

'I'm sure that's not true,' he said softly.

Essie held his gaze and watched his eyes change colour to an azure blue, like the ocean on a postcard. She wondered again about his biology, the chemistry of it. Did the colour mirror his moods? If it was a type of heat reaction, why would it happen now?

As she stared at him, logic and instinct warred inside her. She didn't want to trust him. She'd relied on herself for a long time. Other people always disappointed her, even when they didn't mean to. Look at poor Cecil. He had made her care for him, trust in his friendly, supportive presence, and then he had gone and quietly had a stroke in his back garden. One day, the detective would probably disappoint her too.

I can't go through that again and survive it, can I?

But it was hard keeping a secret for so long. Heavy. Tiring. She knew she could never unburden herself of it, but it would be a relief to share it. And now not only was her father missing, Anna was dead and the killer had been in her house. Plus, an ancient guild of vampires seemed to have her in their sights as well. And even though David could be dangerous – she had seen that with her own eyes – he didn't feel dangerous to her. Somehow, he felt *safe*.

She took a deep breath and picked a place to start.

'It all began when I was finishing my PhD. I was working late one night in the lab. Zion's theory for creating wormholes fell out of fashion after the fifties. But I kept being drawn back to it. The basis of his work, the maths, was still solid. I began to wonder if I could build on it using coding and a new type of machine, a temporal radiometer. It's a quantum supercomputer that controls a large set of magnets. There are only a handful of them in Australia. They have to be used in special laboratories with metal encasing.'

She glanced at his face. He was focussed, listening. She was trying to keep the science high level, make it easy to understand, but quantum physics was a hard sell to lay people. David inclined his head.

'So a bit like how Alexander Graham Bell invented the basic telephone and then technology evolved and about one hundred years later we have the internet?' David asked.

She smiled despite herself. It wasn't the worst analogy. He was trying.

'Sort of, yes.'

'Okay,' David said.

'I played around with the code for months, but I only had a few opportunities to test it. Access to the temporal radiometer is in high demand. As students, we were at the bottom of the pile and had limited lab slots.'

Essie was quiet for a moment, reaching for a way to describe what had happened the last time she'd been in the lab. Even now, it seemed like a wild dream, and she still wondered whether she had imagined it.

'Anyway, I had been researching for months and begun to think it wouldn't work. I had one more scheduled visit in the lab before my thesis was due. One last chance to experiment with the radiometer. As I entered the last line of the code into the computer, behind the glass, where the magnets are, there was a bright flash of light. A wormhole opened.'

Essie stopped, focused on David, tried to gauge his response. His face went blank for a moment, and she felt the knot in her stomach clench.

'I know it sounds crazy. Unbelievable,' she acknowledged quickly.

David grinned back at her. 'As unbelievable as vampires, and gods and monsters?'

She chuckled lightly, relaxing. 'I guess we are in similar territory.'

'Then what happened?' he urged.

'The wormhole was spinning like a little circular rainbow. It was the most beautiful thing I've ever seen. But it began to grow and exert a force.'

'Like a blackhole?' David asked.

'Similar. Blackholes suck objects in and that's it. They're gone. In theory, wormholes should allow objects to go in and out the other side.'

'Like tubes? That's what Zion called them,' David said, referencing their earlier conversation. She nodded appreciatively.

'Exactly. But the larger a wormhole gets, the larger the gravitational field. I could feel the pull of it from behind the glass. I'd been so focused on making it happen, I hadn't given much thought to what next. I started to panic. But then it just collapsed.'

'What happened?'

'The power to the lab went out everywhere. I think I must have flipped a fuse because the wormhole was drawing so much energy into the radiometer.'

David looked at her in complete silence for a moment, then smoothed his hair back.

'So, you solved it? Zion was right. Time travel is possible.'

Essie shook her head.

'No, it's more complicated than that. It's a big leap between opening a wormhole and time travel. Much bigger than the leap between Bell and the internet. The wormhole I created was the size of a twenty-cent piece. It could be made bigger, but a human still couldn't travel through it. They'd be ripped to shreds by the gravitational force. Not to mention, I have no idea where, in time or space, the wormhole would lead.'

David cupped his chin thoughtfully, running his hand over his five o'clock shadow. She made a mental note to ask him about vampire hair growth. She would add it to her list of questions about vampire biology.

'Okay. There's something I don't understand. You made this incredible discovery, but in your dissertation, you said the exact opposite. You told me you proved Zion's Loop couldn't be solved.'

Essie swallowed hard. This was the worst part of the story. The part that made her feel dirty. But there was no going back now.

'I had to lie,' she whispered. 'A few days after the wormhole happened, a woman contacted me. She offered me a lot of money to sell her my work.'

Essie shifted her weight in her seat. She could still hear the woman's voice in her head, feel the cold chill that had descended on her every time her phone rang with that unknown number, the child-like voice on the other end.

'At first, I thought she was just crazy. But she was so insistent, calling me late at night, asking me how close I was to publishing. She didn't want anyone else to have the work. Eventually she said if I didn't help her, then something could happen to me or to someone I loved.'

'Your father?'

Essie nodded dully.

'Why didn't you go to the police?'

'She had threatened my father. She emailed me photos of him at the restaurant, his house. She made it clear she knew his every move, and I believed she was dangerous. If you'd heard her voice, you'd understand.'

'So instead of handing it over to this woman, you faked the results?'

Essie wrung her hands together.

'I didn't know what else to do. I knew it wouldn't be enough to just stop working on it. She wouldn't have left us alone. So, I decided the only way to end it would be to falsify the results in a way that proved the equation was unsolvable.'

'That must have been difficult after what you had achieved,' David said.

'Not as difficult as the idea of my dad being hurt.' Tears stung her eyes, and she wiped at them with her hand before David rummaged around the couch and found the handkerchief. She took it from him again.

'In the end, it was all for nothing anyway. Dad disappeared a few months after I published my results.'

'So you suspect the woman made good on her threats? But why was she so interested in your work? It was obviously very important to her if she was willing to kill for it. If, as you say, it was a theoretical discovery, what was she planning to do with it?'

Essie shrugged. That question had always stumped her too.

'I tried to explain to her that no one could possibly go through the wormhole, that it would need years of testing in a controlled environment with lots of refining to be of any practical value. But she still wanted my work, one way or another.'

'And did you hear from her again after your father disappeared?'

'No. But if she wasn't involved in his disappearance, it's a pretty big coincidence. Dad wouldn't have just left like that. He'd never do that.'

David nodded. 'And why didn't you tell the police about this after he was gone?'

Essie looked away. 'I think I was holding onto the hope that he might still be alive. I know it's stupid, but I thought if I told the truth, it could make it worse for him. And I'd lied to so many people by that point. I knew at the very least my academic reputation would be ruined and I'd lose my job.' A bitter laugh rose out of her chest. She'd ended up losing her job anyway.

David took a silver fob watch from his pocket. He turned it over and over steadily in one hand as he scratched his head with the other. A tightness snaked up her back. She straightened. What would he think of her now that he knew the truth?

'I'm sorry you've been through so much, alone,' he said. 'It can't have been easy keeping all of that a secret.' Essie's eyes found his. He held her gaze with his own. Calm, confident. She felt something curl in her stomach. It wasn't the knot of anxiety she'd carried for so long. It was something new. A few moments passed in silence.

'All right,' David said at last. 'Back to the original question. How does all of this tie you to Anna and her killer?'

Essie cleared her throat. 'Well, we know Anna was looking at Zion's equation. I don't know how, but it's possible she worked out that I had lied in my dissertation and wanted to expose me. Maybe the woman found out as well? Maybe she tried to get Anna to help her too and she refused, so the woman killed her?'

David nodded.

'That makes sense. That could also explain why Anna's killer's scent was in your room – they were looking for proof you had lied. But what I still don't understand is how the Bloodborns are involved.'

'Maybe they are working together?' Essie offered.

'Maybe, but why? Since their numbers and strength have been so diminished over the last century, the Bloodborns exist to feed and cause chaos. They look for ways to destabilise societies and take power. Human trafficking, terrorism, genocides. Science has not traditionally been an interest for them, unless there's more at stake – like a hydrogen bomb.'

Essie frowned. It didn't really add up. Especially since there was no real-world application for her discovery, not yet anyway.

'What about your missing notebook?' David asked. 'You seemed very worried when you realised it was gone.'

Essie's head shot up and she tensed. 'How did you know that?'

'I can hear your heartbeat,' David said, inclining his head at her. 'It was hammering when you opened your bag and found it gone.'

'Oh,' she said, feeling the heat on her cheeks. She cleared her throat as she wondered what else he knew about her she didn't realise.

'What is so important about that notebook?'

She hesitated a moment. Her instinct to withhold was a long held one.

'I wrote it all down in the notebook. All my notes for solving the equation. Half in that book and half in another identical notebook. I know it was foolish. I shouldn't have kept any records. But I didn't want to erase it completely. It was so important to me. And if I ever lost it, the equation was incomplete, held in two separate parts. Turns out that was a good idea.'

David nodded. 'Indeed.'

'The theft had to have been targeted – otherwise it's not obviously valuable. It's strings of handwritten numbers and letters, just like what you photographed in Steenberger's flat. Only a few people would even be able to make sense of it. But what I don't understand is how they would even have known it existed. I didn't tell anyone about it.'

A vibrating noise came from David's pocket. He put his watch away in his breast pocket and fished out his phone. He glanced at the screen before silencing it and placing it on the coffee table.

'Well,' he said. 'Someone worked out you had lied. Then they found out the notebook existed, they wanted it, and now they have it. The question is, what are they planning to do with it?'

Chapter 22

Essie

All the little puzzle pieces floated around in Essie's mind's eye. She mentally rearranged each one, looking for some order or pattern. There had to be a logic to it. They were missing something vital, but what?

'Okay, we know that whoever killed Anna was probably the same woman that threatened you and your father.'

Essie nodded. 'You said the Bloodborns weren't in Anna's apartment. But they were in my house, and they took the notebook when I had the bike accident.'

'Anna's killer must be working with them, and they must have figured out you solved the equation,' David said. 'But what we still don't understand is *why* they wanted it in the first place. They obviously see something in it that we don't.'

That was the crux of it. As exciting as her discovery was for quantum mechanics, if you were a research scientist and not trying to cure cancer, most people didn't care. Even other scientists would often glaze over when she discussed her work. She stood up to brush the biscuit crumbs from her lap and accidentally nudged the coffee table with her knee. Her teacup, perched on the edge, teetered before toppling over. She stretched for it, but David had caught it and replaced it on the coffee table before she could blink. His hand grazed hers as he pulled back. He still felt so warm. She met his eyes and saw the colour had changed back to the usual grey-blue. She was becoming convinced the colour change had something to do with his mood and body temperature. His vampire physiology must affect the biological composition of his irises somehow.

Then it hit her. Almost as hard as smacking her head on the concrete in the laneway.

Of course! Vampire physiology!

She pushed her glasses up on her head and rubbed her eyes, trying to step through it clearly in her mind. Was it possible? Could that be the answer? She inhaled a sharp breath.

'What?' David said, frowning.

'Maybe what the Bloodborns see in my discovery is themselves! I told you before, a human would be ripped to shreds in the wormhole. But a vampire . . .'

He raised his eyebrows at her expectantly as she took another breath, graspsing for the right words to explain her thoughts to him.

'From what I've seen, vampire physiology is much more robust than ours. You have super strength and you're very fast,' she indicated the saved teacup to underline her point.

'You don't physically age. But you're not a reanimated corpse. You still grow hair,' she pointed to his chin, 'and you are warm to the touch, so your heart is still pumping blood.' She reached out and pressed her palm to his chest to confirm her suspicion, and after a moment, she felt it. The strong, steady rhythm of a reassuringly normal heartbeat. She lifted her eyes to his face and realised he was staring down at her. Feeling the heat in her cheeks, she took a step back.

'I'm not a biologist, but I think you are continually regenerating, on a cellular level. Otherwise, your muscles and tissues would have atrophied by now with extreme old age, your organs would have shut down. Whatever makes you a vampire has made your body virtually indestructible. And you share this same basic physiology with the Bloodborns?'

A look of concern passed over David's features and he nodded slowly.

'So what you're saying is, the Bloodborns assume that vampires might be able to travel through the wormhole you created.'

'Can you think of a better reason for their interest in this technology?'

'Immortal creatures with a penchant for chaos seeking the power to travel in time. Imagine what they could do with it,' he said slowly. 'Does anyone else know about the second notebook?'

Essie shook her head. 'I don't think so. I hid it in the

back of the giant filing cabinet in my office at the Institute. But I didn't think anyone knew about the one in my bag either.'

'Well, once the Bloodborns realise that what they have is incomplete, they will be looking for the rest.'

Essie's mind whirred, trying to assimilate her incomplete thoughts.

'They can't know that it's incomplete. They won't understand what to do with it at all. Only a handful of people in the world know. Like I said, it's just numbers and letters to the untrained eye.'

David's phone vibrated again, the glass tabletop amplifying the sound. They both looked down at the caller ID. Detective Morton.

'This is the second time she's rung. I haven't checked in all morning. They'll be starting to get worried,' he said apologetically, putting the phone to his ear.

'Sorrow,' he answered.

Essie watched David's face as he spoke. His brow creased in response to whatever Detective Morton was saying.

'Thanks, Morton. I'm following a promising lead – I'll explain later. But can you let Jefferson know I'm on it?'

He hung up the call.

'We have another problem,' he said, gathering Essie's coat and holding it open for her. She slipped her arms through the sleeves reflexively.

What else could possibly have gone wrong?

'Morton said the coroner's office just rang the station.

Anna Steenberger's body is missing. They aren't exactly sure when it happened.'

Essie frowned at him as she buttoned her coat. 'What do you mean *missing*?'

David pulled his tie back over his head and straightened it.

'You said the Bloodborns would need someone to explain the equation, figure out what to do with it. Could she do it?'

Essie's mouth fell open.

'She's no expert, but she'd probably be able to help. But David, she's dead.'

David raised his eyebrows at her pointedly.

'Maybe.'

A chill moved through Essie's bones and she shuddered.

'You mean she . . . she's one of them?'

'Possibly. She would have had to have some of their blood in her system before she was killed. The Bloodborns had not been in her flat. Rafael double-checked. But that doesn't mean she hadn't met them before, somewhere else.'

Hot anger shot through Essie's body.

'So, she was working with them the whole time?'

David retrieved his coat and keys at vampire-speed before grabbing her by the elbow and urging her towards the door.

'I don't know yet. Come on,' he said, 'we need to get to your office and retrieve the second book. If they do have Anna on their side, it won't take long for them to realise the equation they have is incomplete. We need to beat them to it.'

'But I still have so many questions about all this vampire stuff,' Essie protested as David pulled her through his flat door and steered her towards the elevator.

He tapped the call button. It dinged as the doors slid opened.

'I will answer whatever I can for you. But first we need to stop the Bloodborns from stealing technology that they could use to become immortal time travellers.'

The doors closed and the elevator began to descend.

Chapter 23

David

The Institute buildings stood like rows of monoliths, back lit by the brightness of the setting sun. A rising full moon was already visible on the horizon as Essie directed David to one of the lesser-used parking lots on the edge of the campus.

'Ben took my staff access and office keys when I was leaving. Angela insisted.'

'Why?' David asked, turning off the engine.

'I'm on sabbatical, remember? Well, the provost stood me down due to all the fuss with Steenberger's video.'

'Ah, the video.' David had forgotten about it amidst everything else.

'Yes, though now losing my job seems minor in comparison to time travelling vampires. But it means we might have trouble getting in if my office is locked up.'

'I can probably help with that,' David smiled.

'I thought you were supposed to try to stay incognito?'

He tilted his head and she rolled her eyes at him. 'What did Rafael say?'

David had made a call to the older vampire from the car telling him their plans.

'No one has been back to your place. He wanted to meet us here, to help out, but I told him to wait there.'

He was relieved Raf was staying away for now. The last thing he needed was someone else to watch over. Bloodborns on the loose, in search of the second notebook, was enough to worry about. And then there was Essie. She was determined, but still human. He realised too late he should have thought things through more before bringing her along. He surveyed the parking lot. All seemed quiet.

'What's wrong?' She asked, following his gaze.

'This could be dangerous. It might be better if I go in alone,' he said.

Essie unclicked her seat belt. 'No way. I'm coming with you. You won't be able to find the notebook without me.'

David pressed his lips together and sighed.

'You can explain it to me. If Anna is now helping the Bloodborns, won't they suspect this is the next most logical place to look for your work? They already came up empty-handed at your house. If we run into them here, I would rather you aren't in the middle of a direct confrontation again.'

Essie's face was set. 'Too bad. I'm coming with you,' she said, raising her chin defiantly, her blue eyes intense. 'It's my work that started all this. I have to help.'

His stomach tightened. This was a bad idea. He was about to argue the point further when she spoke again.

'Do you really think they made Steenberger a vampire?'

David looked over at her, trying to gauge her feelings. She had made it clear there was no love lost as far as her relationship with Anna Steenberger was concerned, but the stark reality of seeing her again, reborn, would be something else.

'It makes sense,' he said slowly. 'It would explain her missing body. If the woman who contacted you is working with the Bloodborns, which seems likely, they knew already you wouldn't help them. And, as you said, they need someone with the right expertise.'

Essie's mouth pursed.

'I wouldn't call her an expert. She was trying to figure it out – the drawings in her flat. She must have been working with them before she was killed.'

'Yes, perhaps. Although if that is the case, I don't know why they would have abandoned her body. The crime scene looked more unplanned, like it was an accident and the killer panicked and ran. And as I said, she was definitely killed by a human.'

David unfolded himself from the front seat. He quietly closed the door behind him, leaning up against the car with his arms folded over his chest. Essie rounded the car and stood by his side.

'David, if we do come across a Bloodborn, just so I'm prepared, how do we actually kill it?'

He hesitated a moment before replying to her.

'Beheading is the safest option. It's the only way to be sure.'

Essie screwed up her nose at him.

'But we won't be trying to kill them if they're here. It's too dangerous,' he said, turning his gaze on her. 'We will leave and regroup, understand?'

Essie swallowed hard and nodded. 'Okay.'

'Lead the way,' he said, pushing off the car. If she was so determined to come with him, he would at least keep her in front, where he could see her.

Essie marched off, her blonde hair tucked into the back of her coat, and her hands jammed in her pockets. She led them out of the carpark and headed towards a large grass quadrangle. David scanned their surrounds, all his senses primed.

'Quantum physics is over on the other side,' she said, pointing towards the opposite end of the quadrangle where he recognised the sandstone buildings rising in the distance.

They headed for the entrance, weaving in under one of the giant stone archways holding up the veranda that wrapped around the entire lower floor. Essie turned up the collar of her coat and shivered in the twilight air. David smelled rain on the way.

He tensed as they passed a group of students, hefty textbooks in hand, noisily discussing the lecture they had just left. Essie ducked her head and leaned into David's side.

'Don't worry,' she whispered, 'that was the last class of the day. They'll be gone soon.'

He hadn't even turned his mind to the safety of the students. At least the empty campus would reduce the risk of collateral damage.

They stopped outside a glass door next to a noticeboard littered with advertisements for tutoring services and house mates, contact numbers printed along the bottom on little tear-off slips. It was not the way he had got to her office on his last visit.

'This is the side entrance and largely public access.' She stepped inside and held the door open behind her. David hesitated on the threshold.

'Look, I'm not trying to be difficult, but I would feel much better if you let me go ahead of you now.'

Essie rolled her eyes at him.

'You might have been born last century, but I wasn't!'

He resisted an urge to groan.

'It's not machismo, it's just simple physics. You said it yourself. I'm virtually indestructible. You, on the other hand, are not.'

He pointed at the side of her head, which was still sporting a small lump and a bluish bruise. Appealing to her own logic was a low blow, even if it was the truth. She narrowed her eyes at him, and he breathed out, waiting.

'All right,' she said, standing aside and holding the door for him. 'That makes sense. Up those two flights of stairs, then the second corridor on the right leads to my office.'

David stepped past her. 'Stay close.'

He measured his tread on the stairs carefully to ensure she remained right behind him. When they reached the top, he stopped and scanned the hallway. Essie collided with his back.

'That way,' she said, pointing towards a darkened corridor. Sensing nothing out of place, he continued.

Harsh fluorescent lights flickered to life in sequence overhead as the sensors detected their movement along the corridor. They passed by several empty offices and a tea room before rounding the corner.

They were a few steps down the second corridor when David heard it, the steady thrum of a heart. His outstretched hand caught the sleeve of Essie's coat. But the scent he caught was distinctly human, and one he recognised.

'It's okay, David, it's just Ben.'

Essie's young research assistant sat at his desk, earbuds in, staring down at his phone. Essie stood in front of him, waving her arms about.

'Ben!' she shouted.

He jumped with a start and ripped the earbuds from his ears.

'Oh, my God!' he said breathlessly. 'What are you doing here, Dr Thornton?'

'I need to get into my office, Ben,' Essie said, thumbing in the direction of the office. 'I left something in there, something personal, and I really need to get it back.'

Without waiting for his response, she walked over to the door and took hold of the handle, turning it a couple of times before sighing.

Ben stood up and crossed his arms over his chest. 'You aren't allowed back in there. Provost's orders.'

'Come on, Ben. I'm not here to steal state secrets. I just want to grab one little thing, then I'll go.'

She smiled widely at Ben and he flinched like he'd been hit. His gaze finally landed on David.

'Oh hi,' he said. 'I didn't see you there.'

David nodded in acknowledgment and Ben glanced between him and Essie.

'David drove me here,' Essie explained. 'I had a bike accident.'

'Okay,' Ben said, shrugging. His phone buzzed on the desk, and he reached for it reflexively.

'Ben!' Essie shouted. His eyes snapped back to her, and he slipped the phone in is back pocket.

'Sorry, doctor, you will have to take it up with Aunty. I can't let you in.'

'Ridiculous!' Essie shouted, stomping her foot like a toddler. David resisted the urge to grin and stepped forwards.

'Ben, Dr Thornton has been helping me with my investigation into Anna Steenberger's murder. We need to get something from her office. It might be the key to solving this case.'

'Oh, I heard about that!' Ben said, his eyes suddenly alight. 'Who are the suspects? How was she killed?'

'The investigation is still ongoing. But I would be most grateful if you could assist us with our enquiries. I am quite sure that your aunty would understand, given the circumstances.'

'You obviously never met her,' Ben retorted.

'No, but I know how much she wants Anna's case solved. What we are looking for could be vital evidence.'

Ben sighed and reached for a lanyard of keys on a hook over his desk.

'Okay fine. Just hurry up. I can't lose this job, or I won't graduate this semester.'

He singled out a key from the chain and inserted it into the lock.

'You've got five minutes,' he instructed, swinging the door open for them. 'And if anyone asks, I had nothing to do with this!'

He slumped back down in his desk chair and pulled out his phone again.

David led the way into the darkened office. Essie followed him, flicking the light switch on.

Just as before, there were books, papers and pens strewn carelessly around every surface.

'Everything looks the way I left it,' Essie said, moving quickly to an industrial steel grey filing cabinet behind her desk. 'I don't think anyone else has been here.'

A quick inhale from David confirmed she was right. There was only her distinct scent in the office, the mix of sweet cloves and soap. Although how she could tell nothing had been disturbed amongst the mess was a mystery to him.

Essie nudged a pile of textbooks out of the way with the toe of her shoe. They toppled and fell in a messy pile. David stood near the door, keeping watch.

'The notebook is in a suspension file at the back,' she said, squatting in front of the cabinet. David heard the grind of metal on metal as she wrestled the drawer open. A random assortment of items thumped onto the floor beside her as she tossed them away – old running shoes, a jar of mustard and a tape dispenser.

'Got it!' Essie eventually exclaimed. David turned as she thrust a green notebook over her head.

'Good. Let's go,' he said, glancing back into the hallway.

Essie flicked the light switch off and he pulled the door closed behind them.

'Thanks Ben,' Essie said, passing back the key lanyard. 'For what? I never saw you,' he said, without looking up from his phone.

'Let's go.' David ushered Essie back towards the corridor. An awful thought gripped him. He turned back.

'You should leave for the night,' he said, drumming his knuckles on Ben's desk. 'Go straight home and don't speak to anyone on the way. Police orders.'

Ben sighed loudly.

'All right. I was about to leave anyway.' He put his phone down and started packing away his laptop.

Essie frowned at David as they walked towards the corridor.

'Will he be okay?' she whispered.

'If he does what I told him to.' David hoped it was true. He took Essie by the elbow and lead her back into the corridor.

Chapter 24

Essie

Darkness blanketed the quadrangle when they emerged. Essie had been at the Institute after hours plenty of times, but never like this, sneaking around. She shivered in the night air. Rain fell with increasing intensity, landing in fat drops. Essie caught the fresh smell of petrichor as they skirted the veranda, trying to stay dry. Lightening flashed above, momentarily illuminating the quadrangle.

'We'll have to make a run for it, I'm afraid.' David set his face to the weather. As they reached the edge of the veranda, a roll of thunder burst overhead. Essie tucked the notebook securely inside her coat and reached for David's hand like it was the most normal thing to do. She braced for a dash to the car. Then in the next instant, she had been manoeuvred carefully, but abruptly, against the stone wall behind her.

David was still holding her hand, but his body was pressed flush against hers, a finger placed over her lips. He felt tense, as if his muscles were charged with humming energy.

Essie caught a glimmer of movement in her peripheral vision. It was light, like a butterfly, and obscured somewhat by the darkness. She turned her head towards it, but it was moving too swiftly to track.

Oh no.

A sick feeling settled in her stomach, and she held her breath instinctively.

David pivoted to face the other direction, releasing her hand and sweeping his arm diagonally across her body as he did so, pinning her against the wall with his back to her. A lithe figure appeared in front of them, dressed in black, and with a cap of white-blonde hair cut in an angular bob that framed her pixie face. This was not the vampire from her house. For a start, she was a woman, or maybe a girl. She was small and delicate, and gave off an air of fragile beauty. But judging from the way she moved, and David's reaction, she was most definitely a threat.

'*Bon soir* to you both,' she said, rendering a shallow curtsy, her arms curving as gracefully as a ballet dancer.

Essie's heart shuddered, and the nausea deepened. The tinkly bell quality of the woman's voice was unmistakable. She had heard it enough times, disembodied on the other end of a phone line.

Oh no, not her. It can't be her!

'I am Sabine Alexandrine Sauveterre. How do you do?'

David answered without hesitation. 'Good evening, Ms Sauveterre. Or should I say, *enchante*?'

The woman laughed lightly. '*Enchante*,' she replied,

holding out her slender hand, as if she were a princess in an old-fashioned movie waiting for a handsome suitor to kiss it.

David did not take it. He eyed her steadily.

Sabine huffed in mock sadness, then pirouetted on her toes before coming to rest in a graceful pose.

'It's sad how the modern generation has abandoned the common courtesies of old, don't you agree? And yet they consider themselves so advanced.'

She shrugged her bird-like shoulders and raised her eyebrows at him, but David did not respond.

'No matter. We can dispense with formalities since I already know your names. Let us get right down to business, as they say, *Monsieur Detective*.' She joined her hands together in an attitude of prayer then flexed her long fingers as she moved a little closer to them. Essie felt David's grip on her tighten, almost painfully, as he angled himself between her and Sabine. The other vampire laughed again.

'There's no need to worry for your little human companion. I promise you, no harm will come to her, as long as you give me what I came here for.'

'And what is that?' David asked, not relaxing his grip. As Sabine drew nearer, David's frame completely obscured Essie's view of the blonde vampire. She peeked around his arm.

'Monsieur, don't be coy. We are both too old for these kinds of games,' Sabine smiled, and her teeth glinted silvery white. Essie grimaced as she imagined those same teeth tinged red with blood, sinking into human flesh.

'Where is the vampire you sent to her house? Whatever he was meant to do, he failed, you know,' David mocked her.

Sabine's laughter echoed around the veranda.

'Oh, him,' she said, winking at David. 'Tony!' Even her raised voice was musical.

The dark-haired man who had attacked her in her house appeared from the long shadows and stood a foot away from Sabine. His legs were parted. Essie could make out his thick neck. His middle-aged face was pock-marked with acne scars, salt and pepper hair covered his head. He too was wearing black leather. Maybe the Bloordborns had a uniform code.

'It's hard to find reliable help these days,' Sabine sighed indolently. 'He completely failed to achieve his mission. Still, he'll do in a pinch, I suppose.'

Inclining her head to the side, she met Essie's eyes around David's arm. David's grip tightened.

'I suppose the saying is true. If you want something done properly, sometimes you have to do it yourself,' she smiled, baring her teeth again. Essie's mouth ran dry.

'You will not get what you came for.' David held his ground. Steady and composed.

'Won't I?' Sabine teased. 'But what about Dr Esther Thornton? What is it she came for?'

The mention of her own name sparked a reaction in Essie.

'What do you mean?' she shouted, finding her voice, even if it was trembling.

Sabine smiled coquettishly and tilted her head.

'My poor doctor. All alone. Don't you want to know what happened to your father?'

Essie leaned into David's solid weight. The nausea almost doubled her over. Adrenalin rushed through her bloodstream. Even she could hear her heart, blood pounding in her ears. Her father's soft features appeared before her, shadow-like. She saw his grey eyes smiling, heard him gently encouraging her.

Sabine lifted her face and inhaled deeply.

'How sweet – you still wear his shirt,' she smirked, holding Essie's gaze for a moment before throwing a glance at David. 'And here I thought scientists weren't given to the sentimental.'

Essie looked down at her half-buttoned coat with the checked shirt beneath. It was her father's shirt. She had worn it to the hospital because it was comforting. It felt almost like one of his hugs. But how could Sabine have known that it was his, that it was his scent? Unless . . . *No.*

'Essie!'

It was David shouting her name. She felt his weight shift, and then everything moved quickly in a haze of light.

'Run,' he whispered. She couldn't be sure where his voice had come from because he was not in front of her anymore. But she instantly obeyed him.

As she glanced back over her shoulder, she saw David launch himself at Sabine. Tony stumbled backwards. Essie's whole body clenched. They outnumbered David two to one. After witnessing the altercation in her house, she didn't even count herself as being in the fight. At best, she would be collateral damage, at worst, she would be a liability.

With the adrenalin fuelling her muscles, before she knew it, she was halfway across the quadrangle. The rain was falling in sheets, drenching her hair, the grass squelching softly beneath her with each footstep. Her glasses fogged up with moisture, but she could just make out the carpark on the other side of the quadrangle and gasped in a lung full of humid air as she ran.

Tony appeared in her path. Droplets of rain splashed off his forehead, running down his face. Essie couldn't stop. She ploughed into him, then spiralled backwards. It was like hitting a marble wall. He slashed at her with his outstretched hand, but she managed to pivot away out of his grasp. As she turned, she felt the heel of her boot slip, and she rolled awkwardly on her ankle, falling onto the rain-soaked grass. She willed herself to get up, to move, but her body would not obey. She lay on the ground, paralysed, covering her head with her hands.

The blow she thought would fall didn't come. No one grabbed her and dragged her away. A crashing noise exploded near her head. She couldn't tell if it was the thunder or something else. When she finally dared take her hands away from her face, she adjusted her glasses and looked around. About five metres from where she lay, there were two figures wrestling in the dark. One must have been Tony, but she couldn't make out the other.

'Up!' David was at her side. He grabbed her by the hand, hauled her to her feet.

Essie patted her coat pocket, relieved to still feel the

notebook safely tucked away. She took a step forwards and fell awkwardly towards David. Pain shot up her leg, taking her breath away.

'Damn, my ankle,' she cried out, clutching the sleeve of his coat as his arms closed around her.

He swept her up, cushioning her against his chest. The world blurred past her as he sped towards the carpark.

'I think someone tackled Tony,' she whispered hoarsely, as David set her down next to the car.

'It was Rafael,' David replied, unlocking the car. 'I guess he couldn't help himself.'

Essie balanced on one foot while he opened the front passenger door and lowered her onto the seat.

'We have to go back and help him,' she cried, trying to get out of the car.

David slammed the door shut and was in the driver's seat beside her the next moment. His hair was wet, several strands hung limp across his forehead. But it was his face that made her draw in a sharp breath. He was so pale. The iridescence of his eyes was gone, replaced with a dark red glow. He turned his face away from her and shoved the keys in the ignition.

'What are you doing? We have to go back!' She reached over him, trying in vain to grab the keys.

'No, we do not,' he said, turning over the engine and reversing the car out of the carpark. 'We have to get that notebook as far from here as possible.'

'But what about Rafael?'

David let out a hard laugh. 'Rafael will kill us himself if we go back.'

He raced down the street and took a corner sharply, causing Essie to brace herself against the car door.

'Well, where are we going?' she demanded.

David's hand bristled across his chin, his eyes trained on the road.

'To the police station. It's a public place, there will be other people around. It would be risky for them to come for us there. We can dry off and figure out what to do next. Perhaps get an ice pack for you.'

Essie bent to inspect her ankle. The sharp edges of the notebook jabbed her stomach. She opened the folds of her coat to take it out, placing it carefully on the dashboard. Drops of water fell from her soaked hair onto her shirt, her father's shirt. She became aware she was trembling again, tears running down her face.

'Sabine . . . she was the woman on the phone who threatened me. I'm sure of it. She said she knew about my father . . . she knew this was his shirt . . . but how?'

David reached across to take her hand, squeezing it gently. He glanced at her. His eyes were cerulean blue again, his face not so pale.

'Remember I told you human scents are like fingerprints for vampires?'

He nodded to her shirt. 'That shirt still smells like him, like your father. I didn't realise before because I had never met him . . .'

His voice trailed off uncharacteristically.

'Okay, but Sabine knew. So, she must have met him or taken him . . . hurt him . . . David, *no, no.*' She shook her head.

'Let's not jump to conclusions,' he said, letting go of her hand. 'We don't know anything for certain.'

Essie sniffed back her tears. David was right. Maybe there was another explanation. But she felt like there was something he wasn't saying. His tone was distant.

'What happened to Sabine, David? I couldn't see.'

He shook his head, his brow furrowed. 'I don't know. I lunged at her, and I was sure I hit her, but she was very fast. I heard you scream, and I turned away for a second. Then she was gone.'

Essie glanced in the side mirror but there was nothing there, not even the distant lights of another car. Only the empty, rain-slick road.

'It doesn't make any sense,' Essie said. 'She was there to get the other notebook from me, wasn't she? Why would she just give up and leave?'

David said nothing. His hands gripped the steering wheel tightly as they sped into the night.

Chapter 25

David

The police station was quiet. Most of the day shift staff had gone home. David helped Essie through the glass sliding doors, hobbling beside him as she guarded her tender ankle. He'd barely said two words to her the whole trip. His mind was completely preoccupied. How was he going to tell her about the shirt?

A subtle hint of wisteria washed over him.

'Sir, where have you been? The Inspector's been chasing you all day.' Morton was standing behind the reception desk. She came out to meet them.

David lowered Essie into one of the visitor's seats. 'I've been following up a lead. Dr Thornton's been helping me.'

'We've all been worried about you.' David grimaced. Trouble at work was the last thing he needed in the current circumstances.

'Sorry, I'll be able to explain more tomorrow. Dr Thornton has twisted her ankle though. Could you please get an icepack from the first aid?'

'Okay.' Morton eyed them both curiously before disappearing behind a swipe-access door.

'I think she knows something's up,' Essie said.

David nodded as he lifted Essie's leg onto the adjacent chair. 'She's a good officer. She has good instincts.'

He took off her boot and sock and pushed the hem of her jeans up her calf. She winced as he gently turned her ankle over. It was swollen and turning the colour of eggplant along the lateral side of her foot.

'This looks serious,' he said, frowning. 'Maybe I should take you back to the hospital.'

Essie arched her eyebrow at him.

'There's no time for that! Nothing makes sense.' She leant towards him, her voice lowered. 'Sabine knew who I was, knew we probably had the notebook, but then she just disappeared?'

David nodded. He had to tell her. There was no way around it. But he didn't want to do it out in the open, in the waiting room. They needed some privacy.

'I think Rafael's appearance took her off guard. Perhaps she panicked,' he said.

Rafael. David was more worried about him than he let on to Essie. The chances of the older vampire being a match for Tony were uncertain. Raf had experience on his side, but his physical capabilities were changeable. At full strength, he would be fine, but on a bad day, he couldn't uncork a wine bottle. David tried to push the thought from his mind.

The muscles across his forehead were tight, like his

head was in a vice. What a mess. Essie injured again, Rafael's fate uncertain and Gilbert Thornton . . .

What have you done, Gilbert? And how am I to explain this to your daughter?

'David?'

Essie brought his thoughts back to the moment.

Morton reappeared with the icepack. She wrapped it in a towel and handed it to David. Her eyes had dark circles underneath and she stifled a yawn. David realised with a pang that she had probably been doing extra work, covering for him.

'Did you speak to the coroner about Steenberger?' Morton asked cautiously, glancing at Essie.

'Ah yes. The missing body. Anything further on that?'

Morton shook her head. 'I've never heard of anything like that happening before.'

'I'm going to look into it more,' he said.

'I could help?'

David exchanged a glance with Essie as he wrapped the icepack in the towel.

'Thanks, but it can wait until tomorrow. You go home, Morton. You've been working hard on this case. I'll follow up with the coroner in the morning and we'll regroup with the team to decide the next steps.'

Morton hesitated for a moment.

'All right,' she said, turning to leave. 'I wouldn't mind getting an earlier night.'

'Yes, do that. Good night.'

David collected Essie's boot and sock then helped her

to her feet. He swiped them through the sliding door and led her to his office.

Settling her in the chair opposite his desk, he brought her a towel.

'Thanks,' she said, taking it from him.

She pulled the notebook out and laid it on his desk. They both shrugged off their wet coats, and he looked her over carefully while she dried her hair. Her shirt, her father's shirt, was relatively dry beneath the coat, as were her jeans. Hopefully, she wouldn't catch a fever from being drenched. Apart from her ankle, she seemed otherwise unharmed.

'Take a seat.' He guided her back into the chair and laid the icepack back over her ankle. He picked up the notebook off his desk and flicked it open. It was exactly as she said. None of it made any sense to him. He recognised some of the basic mathematical symbols, but the rest may as well have been written in another language.

All this fuss over some lines of letters and numbers. He sighed.

'I have to tell you something,' he said slowly, closing the book again and putting it back on the desk. Heaviness sat in his chest like a solid weight. He unbuttoned his shirt cuffs and rolled up his sleeves. He started to speak, then stopped, the words seeming to run away as he opened his mouth. Essie looked at him questioningly from behind her glasses and waited.

'Do you remember I told you that human scents are distinctive? No two are alike.'

She nodded. 'Yes, I get it. Your sense of smell is

hyperdeveloped. I've added it to my list of questions to research on vampire biology.'

'You have a list?'

'Yes,' she said. 'I'm saving it up until all of this is over.'

David smiled tightly and nodded.

'Anyway. Scents are utterly unique to each person. Even when humans use perfumes or oils, I can always detect it, somewhere beneath the surface. It's like their essence. That shirt, your father's shirt, it smells sharp and woody, like a pine forest.'

She chuckled. 'That makes sense. He loved nature and being outdoors almost as much as cooking.'

David hesitated again. Essie sighed.

'Look, I know what you're trying to say. The scent on this shirt – Sabine knew it was my dad's because she . . . she took him. I know that he's . . . probably . . . dead.' Her eyes watered.

David's heart clenched. There were no words he could use that would make it any easier.

'Yes, she recognised your father's scent on the shirt because she has met him. But Essie, the scent in Anna's apartment, her killer's scent, it smelled like your father's shirt too. Pine forest.'

She raised her eyebrows at him, blinking. 'Okay. That's weird.'

When he didn't respond, she gave a short laugh.

'But you don't mean? That's ridiculous! Why would Dad have been at Anna's apartment? Maybe you smelt something else, like disinfectant or furniture polish. Half of those are pine scented.'

'Cleaning products have artificial scents. Even humans can tell the difference most of the time.'

She shrugged. 'Well then you must have made a mistake. It's just a mistake . . .'

She stopped abruptly and pressed her lips together. He saw the moment that the weight of it settled over her, that her logic hit a wall. And he couldn't hold her gaze.

'I'm sorry, Essie.'

Essie's hand started to tremble, and her face grew pale. She sat up straight in the chair.

'He would *never* do what you're insinuating.'

David frowned and crossed his arms over his chest.

'I'm not insinuating anything, other than he was in her flat when she died. As I said, it looked like an accident. Perhaps they fought and Anna fell?'

Essie shook her head.

'Why would my father have been there in the first place? He didn't even know her.'

David tilted his head.

'I'm not sure. But we know the Bloodborns are involved. Maybe they forced him to do it because they thought Anna was hiding the rest of the equation? Maybe he's helping them for some reason?'

'No. You're wrong. He wouldn't hide from me all this time, let me believe the worst. He wouldn't hurt a person, even accidentally, and just run away.' Her voice was shaking.

'Not even if he thought he was protecting you? We are all capable of lapses in judgement, Essie. People make mistakes, sometimes ones they regret for a lifetime.'

The scene of the car accident flashed through David's mind again. He heard the little girl's screams. Essie's screams. He reached for her arm but she shrank away.

'Don't touch me!' She said, raising her hands defensively.

Her face was pale, circles of weariness rimmed her eyes. He reached into his pocket and flicked open his pocket watch.

'It's late, Essie. You haven't slept since we left the hospital after . . . Cecil. That's almost twenty-four hours ago. And all you've had to eat in that time are a few biscuits at my flat. You need real food and some sleep.'

Essie was already standing, reaching for her coat.

'What are you doing?'

'I'm leaving,' she said.

'Essie . . .'

'You just accused my father of killing a woman!' Her blue eyes flashed.

'Please, Essie . . .'

'I've known my father my whole life. I met you three days ago. He's not from your world. He's not a killer!'

The words hit him as if she had landed a blow. She staggered towards the desk, scrambling for her notebook. David snatched it from her grasp reflexively.

'Please don't do this,' he said, holding the book away from her.

'Give that to me. It's mine!'

Her face was taut, her eyes wide and unblinking. He could overpower her, of course. Or arrest her. But what good would that achieve? She'd only become more hostile towards him. More angry.

'All right,' he said, passing her the book. She slumped back onto the chair, gripping it to her chest with one hand as she yanked on her sock and shoe with the other.

'Where will you go?' he asked.

She looked away from him, shoving her arms through the sleeves of her coat. She buttoned it up and tucked the notebook inside.

'I'm going home.' He opened his mouth to tell her that was not a safe option but she was already limping towards the door. He moved to block her path.

'I'll drive you.'

'No,' she shoved him against his chest. 'I don't need you. Just leave me alone.' He fell back and let her pass, watching as she hobbled slowly towards the reception.

He trailed her at a slight distance, praying she would change her mind. But he could hear the blood pounding through her veins and he didn't need to be able to see her face to know she was a mess of emotions – anger, fear, disbelief. When she halted at the security doors, he reached around her with his pass to let her out. She stepped through without looking back and made her way to the reception desk.

Slipping his hands into his pockets, he rocked back on his heels as he watched her ask the duty officer to call her a taxi. Should he try to follow her? Would she be safe without him? The doors slid closed and his phone vibrated against his leg. He pulled it out of his pocket.

'Sorrow,' he answered.

The tinkly bell voice on the other end of the phone laughed in response.

'Ah, my good detective. I finally managed to get hold of you.'

'What do you want?' David demanded.

Sabine laughed lightly again.

'We could have had this conversation at the Institute like civilised vampires, but then your friend arrived, and a much better plan occurred to me. Rafael, isn't it? I seem to recall he had another friend before he made you. The lovely Nika. How many years ago was that now? One hundred, two hundred? It all starts to blur together after a century or two. Just like the faces of the Amaranthine I have killed.'

The mention of Nika's name raised the hairs on the back of David's neck. She knew them. She knew about Rafael's past. What else did she know? He forced himself to stay silent, determined not to take the bait. A crunch and a loud, strangled cry issued in the background. *Rafael*. His heart seized.

'Don't touch him!' he threatened. He began walking swiftly back to his office. Sabine only laughed again.

'I'm going to text you the details of a location, detective. Bring me the rest of the code. I don't think I need to spell out what will happen to Rafael if you don't comply. Oh, and do bring the good doctor with you as well. No doubt you have figured out what her poor, deluded father has done, but I have another little surprise for her.'

'This is between us. Leave Essie out of it.'

'If only I could, detective. But she still has a part to

play.' David sank down into his desk chair. Why did Sabine still want Essie? What was she driving at?

'She'll never help you, Sabine. No matter what you do.'

'Is that so? I wonder if you have had the courage to tell her about the accident yet? About what you did? It's a heartless man who can leave a child for dead in the back of a burning car to save his own skin. How do you think she will take that news? Who do you think she will choose to help once she knows the truth? *A bientot*, detective.'

Another loud cry, guttural and pained, punctuated the call, before the line went dead. David stared down at the screen and it flashed with a street name. He put the phone down on the desk and dropped his head into his hands.

Chapter 26

Essie

Essie jolted awake and rolled onto her side. She squinted through the shaft of light streaming through a chink in the curtains of Cecil's lounge room. Her body ached from sleeping, curled up on the tiny couch. She knew David was right. It wasn't safe to go home, and she didn't have a death wish. So, she had directed the taxi driver to drop her at Cecil's, knowing Mary wouldn't have arrived from Greece yet, and that Cecil kept the spare key to his back door under the potted hydrangeas.

A heaviness fell over her as her conversation with David at the police station came back. She only had herself to blame. Trusting him had been a mistake. Hadn't she learnt that lesson in life yet? Other people always let you down, eventually. Although David wasn't exactly a person. But still, how could he accuse her father of something so heinous? Her father wasn't a killer. And he couldn't possibly be working with the Bloodborns, could he?

She heard a soft meow and a warm, furry head bounced against her open palm.

'Moffatt,' she said, stroking his soft coat.

Moffatt mewed again and she pushed off her coat, swinging her legs over the side of the couch. She wiggled her foot carefully. Her ankle was already feeling more supple. She put on her glasses and stood up, tentatively putting some weight down. Moffatt circled her closely as she took a few ginger steps towards the kitchen.

'Are you a hungry kitty?' She asked, rummaging through a cupboard for the cat food. 'Me too.'

She tipped out a scoop of dry biscuits into Moffatt's bowl and glanced around. Everything looked the way it always had. She wasn't exactly sure what she expected. There was no sign of the paramedics having been there, no medical stuff lying around. All Cecil's cookbooks were neatly shelved, his leather reading chair sat in the morning sun by the glass sliding door, his glasses still perched on the arm, as if he were coming back. Essie stared at them for a moment, trying to stop her tears. A part of her wanted to cry, to succumb to her grief for her friend and drown in it. But another part of her was so overcome with the weight of her other problems, including her fight with David and the threat of the Bloodborns, that the two almost cancelled each other out. The result was a kind of numbness.

What had she been thinking leaving David? Whatever he had accused her father of, he was the only one capable of protecting her from the Bloodborns, who were no doubt still searching for her. But her anger and disbelief had got the best of her. She cursed herself for letting her emotions rule her and losing sight of logic.

The ache in her belly pulled her towards the fridge door. She dragged out a hunk of cheese and some wafer biscuits from the cupboard and sat down to eat. Her notebook lay on the kitchen table beside her dead mobile phone. She picked it up and plugged it into the charger on the kitchen bench. The screen lit up with the red half-battery sign, telling her it would need some time to come back to life. She sighed and popped a slice of cheese and a wafer in her mouth.

Then it happened. In the corner of her eye, she caught the flurry of colour, as delicate as butterfly wings, and so fast it would have been easy to miss. A tiny, vibrantly-coloured bird emerged from a hole in the wooden retaining wall and danced its way to a nearby hellebore. Moffatt noticed it too, slinking over to the glass to sit and watch. Essie stared, transfixed by its delicate beauty. It was a pardalote. *Cecil's pardalote.*

'He wasn't exaggerating, was he Moffatt? They are amazing.'

Wheet-wheet, she heard the bird call and immediately an answering call, *wheet-wheet*, from another direction. The bird's mate flittered into view and alighted on the potted hydrangeas by the back door. Moffatt made his move, leaping at the glass with such ferocity it startled her. Moffatt fell back against the tiled floor, licking his wounds. Essie leaned over and patted his head.

'Oh Moffatt, you poor thing. Are you ok?' She patted him gently.

Moffatt raised his head to her voice momentarily and then continued licking.

'What are we going to do without him, Moff? I don't suppose you want to come and live with me? Keep me company?'

The cat swung his grey tail and leapt onto the armchair, curling up contentedly. Essie wished she could do the same. The brief hours of sleep she had managed to eke out between 1:00 a.m. and sunrise had been broken and inadequate to counter the events of the past three days. She knew she looked a wreck, not to mention she was wearing the same clothes she had worn for the last twenty-four hours. They had been soaked in rain, mostly dried out, and then slept in. She plucked at the fabric of the checked shirt, her father's checked shirt, and quickly undid the buttons.

Grabbing a towel from the linen press, she waited for the water to run hot and slid under the shower. Emerging clean and refreshed, she stood in front of Cecil's wardrobe and opened it. It was full of rows of pressed, clean shirts. The organisation reminded her of David and his three-piece suits. She imagined his wardrobe would be as fastidiously tidy. Fingering through the hangers, she stopped on a blue-and-white-collared shirt she had seen Cecil wear at work. She shrugged it over her head without undoing the buttons and dragged her jeans back on. Cecil's shirt swamped her even more than her father's shirt, but it was dry and clean. She inspected the dark bags under her eyes in the mirror on the back of the cupboard door. Her hair was even more messy than usual, strands loose from the low bun. Sighing at her reflection, she went to close the door, but something caught on the bottom of it. She bent to have a closer look and noticed a gift bag that had edged its way out of the wardrobe. The tag had her name on it. Hot tears sprung to her eyes, and she held her breath for a moment.

She wandered over and sat down on the edge of Cecil's bed, bag in hand, and peered into it. Nestled in some white tissue paper was a gold chain with a pendant. She lifted it from the bag and held it in her palm. The pendant was a charm representing a tiny, golden bicycle. She turned it over in her hand, marvelling at the delicate details. The tears slid down her cheeks, and she tasted their saltiness. She slipped the chain over her head and patted it against her chest. Pulling out a card from the bag, she opened it with shaking hands.

Dearest Essie,

They say it's hard for old dogs to learn new tricks. I say it's hard for old men to make new friends! That's what makes our friendship so important to me. And because you're important to me, I have to tell you this.

You are the most gifted scientist I have ever known. Your intellect is unmatched. But that is not all you are. You are brave and kind and loyal. And you shouldn't be an island. I know how terrifying this is, believe me. It would be so much easier not to trust, not to risk ourselves, to stay where it's safe. People can hurt us and let us down. Eventually, they might even leave us. Loving others is always a prelude to grief. Losing my

Sarah taught me that. But she also showed me that it is still worth it. I know this with all my heart.

This necklace is your reminder not to be an island, not to close yourself off to life. Be open to trusting, to looking for the good in people, to forbearing, even with foolish old men who try to show you how to change a flat bike tyre when you already know perfectly well how to do it yourself. You may not have needed him to change your tyre, but he really needed to talk to you. I changed your tyre, but you changed my life. And if you open yourself up, you never know who you might meet, or who might have been waiting all this time, just to meet you.

Yours always,

Cecil x

Essie crushed the card to her heart and wept. *Cecil, Cecil, dear sweet Cecil*. He thought that knowing her was a gift, but he was so wrong. He was the true gift, and she never got to tell him. How would she ever repay him? Every part of her ached with his absence. She rocked herself gently for a few moments, releasing her grief at last.

A loud ping echoed from the kitchen. Her phone was back online. She wandered back to the bench and picked it up. There were new messages from unknown numbers, but only two this time. The first read:

They have R. I'm going after him. Find somewhere to hide and stay safe. I'll find you after. David

Her stomach tightened. So Sabine had taken Rafael from the Institute. It explained why she had left. She had a hostage. She had the bait she needed to lure them into her territory, where she would have the upper hand.

The second message was a street name and a simple instruction.

Bring the code or they die.

Her legs trembled, and she sank down at the kitchen table. At least Sabine got straight to the point. But they who? Who did she have besides Rafael? Nausea gripped her as she imagined David falling into Sabine's grip. She clicked the street name and her phone brought up a map. The address was somewhere on the edge of the city, to the north, in the industrial zone. There wasn't much there. Some abandoned warehouses and buildings. She vaguely recalled that there had been a zoning dispute over the land. The head of a real estate company was on the news ranting about his development application being bogged down in a government planning committee. For now, the area was isolated and derelict. Probably the perfect hideout for a bunch of bloodthirsty vampires.

She and David were obviously being drawn into a trap. The Bloodborns didn't get what they wanted at the Institute, but now Sabine knew they were coming and would be ready. But ready to do what? What was she planning to do with Zion's Loop?

It would be easier to walk away, to not risk herself. If you don't get involved, you can't get hurt. She squeezed her eyes closed and saw David's face. She had never known anyone like him. His strange but captivating eyes. His gentle strength. She remembered how it had felt when his warm hand was holding hers. She glanced down at her scars and swallowed hard.

I don't want to feel this way.

But walking away was no longer an option. She might not be a centuries old Amaranthine vampire sworn to defeat the Bloodborns, but her discovery had drawn Sabine's attention and led to her father's disappearance, to Anna's murder, to Rafael being held hostage and to David risking his immortal life. Whatever her father had done, she had to face it. If he was a murderer, she had to know why.

She carefully tucked the bicycle pendant into the collar of Cecil's shirt. It felt cold against her skin. But the weight that had been sitting on her chest lifted and she drew in an easy breath for the first time in what felt like ages.

'Cecil was right, Moff. I can't be an island anymore. I don't want to be. David is facing some dangerous odds. I don't know how I can help him, but I have to try.'

Shrugging on her coat, she picked up the notebook and tore out the several pages of code, rolled them up, and stuffed them into her bra. As she passed through the kitchen, she remembered David's words about the Bloodborns. *'Blood is an addiction for them.'* She opened a drawer and selected a small paring knife, gently pressing the blade with the tip of her finger to make sure it was sharp. Satisfied it would do, she slipped it up her sleeve.

Moffatt meowed at her from the armchair.

'I'll be back for you. Keep an eye on those birds while I'm gone,' she said over her shoulder as she stepped out the front door and pulled it closed behind her.

Chapter 27

David

David scanned the deserted street of the run-down industrial area in both directions. He had been there once before for a homicide case. A squatter had died from an overdose in the warehouse behind where he was standing. The council responded by erecting large metal fences on the perimeter to keep people out. Now the grass had grown up through the chain link and bits of rubbish had collected in the gaps.

Sabine wasn't in the warehouse. The address she had messaged him matched the old stone church on the opposite side of the road. It was a more fitting location. Looming sinisterly in the distance, it may as well have been a haunted house from a storybook. Ivy weaved its way up the outside walls, the green leaves turning to murky brown the higher the vine climbed, reminding David of gangrenous fingertips reaching for the roof. The window masonry, which would once have held stained-glass panels, was now boarded up with rotting MDF planks. The heavy wooden doors at the church's entrance were greyed and weathered while weeds and overgrown rosebushes clustered around the front steps.

He raked his hand through his hair and straightened his tie. He'd fed again and gained back his strength. But tactically speaking, he couldn't think of many worse scenarios than solo breaching a building where your enemy was expecting you and holding a hostage. Add in the fact that the enemy was a centuries old vampire, and that there were possibly younger and more unpredictable vampires in the building, and things were even more complicated. At least Essie had left him.

Essie. Essie. Her angry words to him. The hurt he saw in her eyes when he had told her about her father's shirt. He tried to push thoughts of her from his mind and focus. Maybe it was for the best she had left. She wouldn't have agreed to wait in the car. Wherever she was had to be safer.

He flexed his hand around the weight of his old broadsword and tilted it. Light glinted off the blade. It had been a while since he had held the sword, much less used it. But it was still sharp. Still capable of cleaving a head from shoulders. Capable of killing a vampire. He sheathed it at his side.

There were myriad ways the scenario he was walking into could play out. He knew already from the confrontation at the Institute he was no physical match for Sabine. Rafael's surprise attack on Tony had thrown her momentarily, but he would have no such distraction this time. This time, he was on his own. He didn't have the advantage of surprise or numbers either. He really didn't have any advantage at all. But his oldest friend was in that church. And he had taken an oath, a long time ago, lying in the cold, crimson-coloured snow. Vows still meant something to him. Promises should be kept. Everything he had been through with Rafael until now was an apprenticeship to this moment, and he wouldn't fail his master. He straightened and set his face towards the church.

A rumble of thunder burst over his head and a flash of lightning tore through the sky. The rain would arrive soon. He could smell it. Well, there was no point waiting any longer. Crossing the road in a blur, he charged his shoulder into the church doors, tearing them from their hinges and sending them spearing into the nave with a loud crash.

No point sneaking around when they know you're coming.

The church's entry way smelled damp. Urine emanated from the carpet, but the smell of dead flesh, of Bloodborns, rushed over him like a torrent. He swallowed back bile and kept moving. Then a throaty cry rose in the distance. A cruel, awful noise.

Raf.

David's muscles tensed, anger burning in him.

He stepped into the nave and blinked. A single, giant flood light, mounted on a tripod in the altar's corner, harshly illuminated the inside of the church. Musty, heavy curtains in various states of shabbiness hung across some of the windows. Beneath the stench of Bloodborns, there was a strong odour of stale cigarette smoke mingled with marijuana and bleach. In the middle of the altar was a floor to ceiling metal cage that glinted on and off with pulses of electricity. Mounted over the altar was what looked like a giant black stone. To the left of the metal cage was a woman, her red curls loose and disarrayed around her head. Anna Steenberger glanced at David briefly, but seemingly undisturbed by his appearance, she turned back to a small table with a laptop on it.

Sabine was leaning against the right of the metal cage, entirely clad in black leather, including thigh-high black stiletto boots, which made the shock of her platinum bob even more contrasting. Her lips tightened to a sneer as she met David's eyes, and she casually twirled the end of a piece of rope, tapping her stiletto loudly. Next to her stood another Bloodborn. A callow youth with sandy-coloured dreadlocks and a snake tattoo on his arm. Anna's ex-boyfriend Jono. The poor young man had lost the scent of engine oil and sweat. Now he reeked of the characteristic smell of Bloodborn.

David let out a loud gasp as he took in the centrepiece of this bizarre scene. A body was mounted on a wooden frame right in front of the cage, below the altar staircase. On the rack, which stood a little over two metres high, was Rafael, stretched out and tethered by metal chains that held his feet and hands in a star-shape. Small metal spikes covered the rack, several protruding through Raf's naked torso at odd angles. His bloodied and bruised face was streaming with sweat, and pools of blood had gathered and congealed on the floor beneath him. David squeezed his hands into fists at his side.

Sabine laughed lightly, the church's cavernous

acoustics causing the sound to echo, giving the impression she was in several places at once.

'You finally made it, *mon cher* detective, and not a moment too soon! I was starting to feel a little sense of *ennui*.' She raised her eyebrows at him and her mouth twisted into a slanted smile.

'But where is the good doctor?' she asked, glancing behind him. 'I am sure I asked you to bring her along.'

'She's not coming, Sabine.'

The vampire turned her violet-grey eyes to Rafael. She gave the rope a tight flick, causing the wooden frame to make a clicking sound. The rack dropped backwards a notch, yanking the metal chains holding Rafael's limbs even further apart. He cried out as his head lolled from side to side.

'Stop it! Let him go!' David cried.

'Do you like my little device? I had it brought here especially for the occasion. After what Rafael did to poor Tony, it seemed a fitting penance. It's not that Tony was particularly dear to me, but an eye for an eye and all that. Or a head for a head, perhaps?' She sighed, stroking the wooden frame fondly, as if it were a lover.

David sped in Rafael's direction, but Sabine was in front of him in an instant. Tearing the broad sword from his waist, she tossed it into a darkened corner of the church.

'I don't think so, detective. You will give me the remainder of the code, or I will kill him.' She yanked on the rope again, eliciting another cry from Rafael.

David met her eyes with his own steely resolve, his mouth tight with emotion.

'I don't have it.' Sabine inclined her head and raised her silvery eyebrows.

'Is that so? No matter. I'm sure the doctor will be along with it shortly.'

David's chest tightened. Essie wasn't coming to the church. She couldn't. She didn't know the location.

'Oh, I see,' Sabine laughed. 'You thought you were the only one who got my little message. Silly detective! I've been around far too long to leave anything to chance. I always have a backup plan.'

It didn't matter if Essie had received Sabine's message. She wouldn't come. She was angry with him. She didn't want anything to do with him, did she?

'Essie's not coming, Sabine. This is over. Let Rafael go.'

'Oh, detective,' Sabine cooed. 'You underestimate the doctor. I have no doubt she will be here soon. I'm sure she's *dying* to find out what happened to her dear father. She never could resist a mystery. That's how all of this started.'

'What did you do to Gilbert Thornton?'

Sabine grinned. 'All in good time! Let's not ruin the surprise for the doctor.'

'Jono,' she said, beckoning him over. He came as obediently as a trained dog. 'Hold this.' She passed him the end of the rope.

'Anna, is everything ready?'

Anna glanced up at Sabine's question, her face triumphant.

'The temporal radiometer is all set up and the Faraday cage will buffer the gravitational field. I've entered the first half of the code, now we just need the rest.'

'*Tres bien!*' Sabine said, turning her attention back to David. 'It is incredible what one can buy online detective, if you have the money!' she said, spreading her hands expansively towards the equipment. 'Special machines and giant magnets, delivered to my door with a few simple clicks. There are some advances of the modern times that I truly appreciate.'

The giant spotlight, all the scientific apparatus, and Rafael mounted near the altar created a bizarre tableau – a mix between a circus, a science fair and a religious procession.

David flinched as the atmosphere in the church shifted. The air shimmered with tension and he heard the sound a microsecond before hungry eyes whipped towards the church entrance – the *thump-thump* of a human heart. It was beating fast, like a bird's wings, and accompanied by the scent of sweet cloves and soap. His jaw tensed.

Sabine shifted her weight, eyeing the younger vampires warily.

'Now Anna and Jono, my little love birds. Remember our talk. The doctor is not dinner. Not yet. We still need her help.'

Anna's lips pulled away from her mouth in a snarl and she gripped the edge of the radiometer, as if anchoring herself by sheer willpower. Jono turned his body towards the entrance and his tongue darted out to moisten his lips. How much control could Sabine still exert over the younger vampires? Would they harken to her words?

Essie stood in the doorless nave, her eyes wide as she took in the scene before her. Her blonde hair was damp, falling in waves over her shoulders, and her glasses were misted with moisture. She lifted one foot and began carefully picking her way through the scattered debris left by David's earlier dramatic entrance. The wooden doors had collided with what remained of the back rows of church pews. Splintered pieces were scattered across the floor, mingled with the rubble of the crumbling flagstone, rubbish, glass, and rusted metal work.

Sabine appeared in Essie's path with a gentle whoosh.

'Finally, doctor,' she said, reaching out a slender hand to caress Essie's cheek. Essie recoiled, her eyes finding David's.

'I hope you brought the code?'

Essie shrugged, her gaze flitting to the wooden structure holding Rafael's maimed body.

'Maybe,' she said, swallowing hard. 'Let him down first.'

'No, I'm afraid that's not how this works,' said Sabine. 'Jono – find it!'

Jono obeyed his mistress, marching towards Essie. He reached for the front of her coat, but she raised her hands in surrender.

'All right,' she said, undoing the buttons. 'Here – take it!'

She extracted a crumpled piece of paper from the front

of her shirt. It had been folded several times over into a tiny square. She shoved it into Jono's fist.

David threw Essie a questioning look. Why would she have brought the second half of the code here and just handed it over?

Jono gave the square of paper to his mistress, and she unfolded it carefully.

'Watch them,' she instructed, sauntering over to Anna. The new vampire stood rooted to the radiometer, but her eyes were firmly fixed on Essie. Sabine thrust the paper in front of Anna. With measured concentration, Anna took it in both hands and studied it carefully for a moment before her face dissolved into anger.

'It's still incomplete,' she shouted, her eyes returning to Essie.

'Well done, Steenberger,' Essie replied. 'I'm impressed.'

In a flash of red, Anna had closed the distance to Essie, and her hand was wrapped securely around Essie's throat. David tensed to move, but Sabine was much faster. Moving as soundlessly as a feather, she separated Anna from Essie before David could even blink.

'All I wanted was for you to acknowledge me, just once,' Anna growled, struggling against Sabine's hold. 'But you see me now, don't you!' Essie fell to her knees, clutching at her throat, sucking in air.

'Enough,' Sabine shouted, tossing Anna against the stone wall with a harsh thud. Anna sagged to the floor, and she scowled darkly at Sabine. David sped to Essie's side and gripped her gently by the shoulders.

'I am *so* tired of your petty human grievances.' Sabine's

voice had lost its melodic quality. She straightened her leather jacket and folded her arms over her chest, glaring down at Anna.

'If the good doctor is going to help us complete the experiment, we will need her to be breathing. For now.'

'Are you all right?' David asked urgently, helping Essie to her feet. She nodded, narrowing her eyes at Anna while she rubbed at her sore neck.

'What are you doing here?' Her blue eyes softened under his gaze.

'I'm sorry for what I said before.'

He shook his head. 'There's no need to apologise. I understand. But you should have stayed away. I can't protect you here.'

She laid her hand on his and smiled. 'It's not all up to you, you know. I still have some tricks up my sleeve.' She inched the cuff of her coat back to reveal a shiny, sharp object.

He frowned at her. How was that tiny blade going to help?

'Now,' Sabine broke in. 'Dr Thornton, if you'll be so kind as to join Ms Steenberger at the computer and finish the code, we will get the experiment underway.' She gestured towards the altar. Anna got up and straightened her hair as she made her way back to the laptop.

'I'll only do it if you let Rafael down,' Essie said again. David's heart jumped and he squeezed her arm, urging her to be silent.

'You're not in any position to bargain, doctor,' Sabine

replied, picking up the end of the rope attached to the torture rack.

'Yes, I am. You just said you can't kill me because you need my help. I won't help you unless you let him go!'

David arched against the sudden pain in his back as Sabine slammed into him like a pillar of marble. Essie was torn away from him as Sabine crushed him against the rack below Rafael's inert body. The end of the rope that had been in Sabine's hand was now wrapped firmly around David's neck and his hands were pinioned in place.

'I'm losing my patience, Esther! Start the experiment now, or I will pull this rope so tightly that the detective's head will pop right off his shoulders.' She tensed the rope around her hand and tugged firmly. David choked out a low growl.

Essie winced, raising her arms. 'Stop, don't hurt him!'

David met her eyes questioningly. She had implied she had some kind of plan.

Dear God, don't let her do anything foolish.

'I'll start it. Just don't hurt him,' she said, sounding defeated.

'Now there's a good doctor.' Sabine's small mouth twisted into a wry smile.

'Jono – over here!' Jono appeared at Sabine's side. 'If the detective moves, pull this tighter,' she said, handing him the end of the rope. Jono secured it, twisting it tightly around his hand.

Essie dragged her gaze from David and slowly made her way to the radiometer.

No, no. Don't give it to her.

He tried to shout to Essie, but the rope was coarse around his neck, crushing his windpipe. Sabine shot a look at Anna and the younger vampire moved back from the consol. Essie plucked the creased notes from Anna's hand and smoothed them out on the table. He heard her breathe deeply as she began tapping away on the keyboard.

There was a loud whir, and the Faraday cage began arcing with electricity, a blue light emanating outwards into the hollow church. Anna and Sabine both looked up, but Essie kept her head down, as if she had been expecting it. What was she planning? How could he buy her more time?

'I'm curious about something, *mademoiselle*,' said David, his voice a strangled whisper. 'Why are you doing this?'

Sabine laughed, a short, bitter sound.

'Over the centuries, the humans all but forgot the vampires. They consigned us to legend and storybooks with everything else that their science could not explain. But I survived, hiding in the shadows, watching, waiting.'

'To what end?' David replied. 'You've walked the earth for hundreds of years, but it has taught you nothing about the meaning of life.'

Sabine pivoted. She snatched a metal spike from the surrounding debris and skewered David, driving the end straight through his middle. He cried out, clutching at his stomach, as his vision blurred.

'What do you know about the meaning of life?' she snarled. Her delicate features dissolved into ugly fury.

David met her gaze, her grey-violet eyes now red, the pupils fully dilated.

'You took your oath to the Amaranthine a mere century ago and you dare to lecture me on the meaning of life! When Enki made us, the world was newborn. Millennia have passed since then and I have watched the humans pollute it and squander the days they were given over and over. The Bloodborns will make better use of their lives than they ever could.'

She gestured to the radiometer. 'This machine will make it possible. The losses of the past, my losses, can be regained, and the Bloodborns will at last fulfil their destiny.'

She took a step towards David and pounded her fist into the metal spike with precision, driving it deep into the wooden structure behind him. Pinned like a moth, he cried out again. He caught Essie's glance, but only for a moment. The muscles in her jaw twitched and a sheen of sweat was visible across her brow. If she was going to do something, he hoped it would be soon.

'I . . . must . . . admit I'm disappointed in you, Sabine.' David's words came in gasps, laboured and shallow. 'You've had millennia to think it over and yet you maintain the same clichéd motivation of every villain in *human* history. Power, greed, ambition. Not . . . very . . . original.'

He winced as the bones around his left eye cracked, splintering under Sabine's fist. She slashed at his torso in a frenzy, tearing his shirt from his body. His chest heaved, and he choked up fluid, tasting blood and bile in his mouth. It spilled down onto his chin as his shattered eye socket quickly swelled, obscuring his vision.

In the distance, Essie's screams echoed. David tried to focus, looking for Essie on the other side of the altar. But his good eye was clouded with blood and sweat, and his head dropped to his chest in exhaustion. He could still hear her heartbeat though, *thump-thump*. It was hammering so fast now, the blood racing through her veins, like quicksilver. Anguish flooded every ounce of his being as his mind dragged him back to the darkest night again, the night in the rain, the night of the car accident, the night he had failed to save her.

'Stop it! You're going to kill him!' Essie's voice was pained and pleading.

'Don't be ridiculous, dear doctor,' Sabine said. 'He's already dead!'

I'm sorry. I'm sorry. He breathed to himself. *Sorry I failed you, Rafael. Sorry I failed you again, Esther Thornton.* The silence seemed to stretch for the longest moment. Then he heard a strange sound. The subtle *shing* of steel on fabric.

'Well, I'm not dead.' It was Essie. 'I'm very much alive.'

He dragged his head up in time to catch the flash of the blade in her hand. Time seemed to contract and slow as she ran the sharp edge of the knife along the pad of her index finger.

The atmosphere in the church crackled like a pile of dry leaves set on fire as the tang of Essie's blood hit the air. An invisible energy pulsed through the hollow sanctuary carrying with it the primal call of hunger. And the eyes of three ravenous Bloodborns all fell on her.

Sabine recovered first. Within a second, she had regained control of herself. But Anna and Jono, the newly turned vampires, were transfixed on Essie. Or more precisely her bloodied finger. Sabine calmly ordered them to stand down, but neither of them seemed to see or hear her, caught in a maelstrom of sensory overload.

David didn't waste a second of their distraction. He launched himself forwards, passing the length of the metal spike through his body. He staggered free and then straightened up. Working quickly, he released the mechanism holding Rafael's body across the wooden frame. Untying his friend's arms, he lifted him down and carried him to a dim corner of the nave, lying him gently on the stone floor.

'*Dado*,' Rafael breathed heavily, his hand on David's arm. 'You should not have come.'

'There's no way I'd abandon you, Raf.' David said, glancing behind him at Essie. 'Will you be all right?' He propped Rafael against the wall. The older vampire's shredded shirt was blood-soaked, but his wounds had already begun to heal.

'Yes, yes. Do not worry about me. You must get the doctor out of here. Sabine knows about us, about Nika. She's trying to undo the past, get back something or someone she loved.'

David turned at the sound of Sabine's voice. She screamed Jono's name. The young man turned his body towards her with great effort, but his eyes remained fixed on Essie, and the blood pooling at her feet.

Anna moved closer to Essie, circling her. The strain of

her hunger was all over her face, but Sabine was blocking her path.

Jono bent his knees into a crouch, poised like an animal ready to attack. David whooshed to Essie's side as Jono sprang forwards. He thrust her out of the way with one hand and deflected Jono with the other. Sabine swooped towards Essie in the same moment, colliding with Jono as he was airborne from the force of David's blow. Both vampires crashed to the ground, falling heavily onto the stone.

David sprang on to Sabine's prone body. Driving his knee into the small of her back, he wrapped the rope around her delicate neck several times before jamming the metal pole straight through her spine. He searched about him for something sharp enough to take off her head.

Anna advanced on Essie and pinned her against the control panel. In David's peripheral vision, Jono lay motionless. The Faraday cage behind them arced again, the noise of the electricity growing louder and louder. Little whirlpools of air eddied across the floor of the cage and beyond, stirring up piles of paper and rubbish in their wake. A vortex coalesced in the middle of the cage. It gave off light like a prism dangling in sunlight. Essie's wormhole. It was working.

Anna lunged at Essie, fangs bared. David tensed and in an instant, his hands had encircled Anna's neck, hurling her against the wall in a tumble of red curls. He turned to face Jono. The newly born vampire was no threat to him, but he was not certain how long Sabine would stay pinned down. Anna was already getting back up. Fighting on multiple fronts while trying to protect Essie was not ideal. His mind tripped through plausible exit strategies. Each one held risks. And they had to make sure the wormhole was closed. Permanently.

The sound of another human heartbeat took his attention. It was barely audible over the increasing noise of the Faraday vortex. It wasn't Essie's heart. It was slower and quieter than Essie's, but still perceptible.

'Stop!' The reedy voice came from the altar.

A stooped man with greying, sparse hair emerged from behind the cage. He wore a knitted beige cardigan over a crumpled checked shirt. The man's face was lined but familiar. David had stared at that face many times as he pored over the missing person's file on his desk. He knew the features well. A long nose, slightly bulbous on the end, bushy blond-grey eyebrows that framed a pair of cerulean blue eyes. The same blue eyes shared by the woman standing next to him.

Chapter 28

Essie

Essie followed David's keen gaze as he looked towards the altar stairs, but she struggled to make out exactly who was standing there. *Cecil?* He had the same narrow shoulders and greying hair as Cecil. He also took each step one at a time, with a careful shuffle. But something was off. Cecil was taller and more rounded. He always used his walking cane. He dressed smartly, his shirts pressed. Cecil was also dead. Essie had watched him die in that sad emergency room. She squinted through her glasses.

No, no. They couldn't have gotten to him, could they? Cecil can't be a Bloodborn!

The noise of the Faraday cage echoed through the church. Essie reached behind her to power it off. She forced her eyes to focus on the man who was now saying her name. As he came into focus, everything else faded to a watery reflection and her reality contracted to a tiny pinpoint of existence.

'Ess,' the man said. He was smiling at her, and there was something familiar about that smile.

With trembling legs, Essie stumbled forwards a step. Was it even possible? She so desperately wanted it to be him. Didn't she?

'Ess!' he said, again.

She opened her mouth to speak, but her tongue was dry and thick. It took several attempts to get the word out.

'D-Dad?' she managed, in a strangled whisper.

The man was standing in front of her. He extended shaking arms. She moved towards him mechanically, allowing herself to be drawn into his embrace.

'I missed you so much,' he said softly. Essie breathed in, the familiar scent of her father filling her senses. David was right. Pine forest, spices. Every visceral memory came rushing back.

Sabine's silvery laugh jolted Essie back into her body. The church came into focus, and she moved away from her father. Sabine stood in front of the Faraday cage, frowning as she held out her leather jacket. It had a large hole in the back where David had pinioned her.

'Oh, it's ruined,' she said with a wry smile, tossing the jacket aside. 'And it was my favourite!'

Essie watched the scene unfolding before her in slow motion, as if it was happening to someone else.

'Welcome, *Gilbert*.' Sabine pronounced her father's name in the French way, keeping the 't' silent. 'It's your dearest daddy, doctor. Don't you have anything to say?'

Essie's stomach curled as a sense of dread washed over

her. She stood motionless, still trying to comprehend what she was seeing.

'Dad, what is going on?' she asked.

Her father turned to her, a broken smile on his face.

'What are you doing here? Where have you been, Dad?'

He gently patted her cheek. 'I am sorry for disappearing on you, Ess. But you will soon understand that it has all been worth it.'

'What do you mean? What has all been worth it?'

Her father smiled and raised his hand, gesturing around the room.

'All of this. Bringing you here today with the help of my friend Sabine.' Essie's mouth fell open as she digested his words.

'Friend? She isn't your friend, Dad. She's a vampire! They are all vampires. Well, one of them used to be my PhD student, but now she's a vampire too!'

Gilbert shook his head. 'I know, Essie. But you don't understand. Soon you will!'

The Faraday cage came to life again. Anna was back at the console typing away. The vampire with dreadlocks, who Sabine called Jono, stood next to her. The wormhole reappeared quickly inside the cage, and in a matter of seconds, it had doubled in size, the rainbow of colours spinning faster and faster every time it dissolved and reformed. It looked exactly like it had in the lab, only brighter and sharper. Essie took a step back and felt David's hand on her arm. A reassurance.

'I knew you could do it. Didn't I always tell you that curiosity was your greatest gift?' Her father clutched his closed fist to his heart as he spoke. Essie frowned at her father. Speechless, she turned to David. He smiled tightly and moved slowly past her.

'Gilbert, I'm David Sorrow,' he said, extending his hand.

'I know who you are, Sorrow,' her father spat. 'You and your friend Rafael.'

Rafael. Where was Rafael? David had rescued him from the rack. But now she couldn't see him anywhere. David angled his body between her and her father.

'If you know about Rafael and me, then you also know why I'm here. And why I cannot let Sabine succeed.' His voice was calm. Composed.

Gilbert chuckled lightly and gestured at the Faraday cage.

'Yes I know why you're here. But *my daughter* has already succeeded,' Gilbert said, smiling. 'It's just as Sabine promised.'

He stared at the Faraday cage, glassy-eyed, mesmerised by its dancing lights.

'Sabine found me not long after you published your dissertation, Ess. She explained everything, that she had tried to help you with your work, but you had refused. You always were so stubborn and independent. At first, I didn't believe her, but she knew so much about everything. And I was so tired of being alone.'

'No, Dad, I—' Essie took a step towards him but felt David's warning hand on her arm.

'Sabine suspected you covered up the truth about your wonderful achievement. At first I didn't believe that. You always had so much integrity about your work. Then Anna agreed to help us. We decided to ask you again. And when I saw the video, I knew immediately you were lying. Your lip quivered and you bit down on it, just like you used to do when you were little.'

Essie's fingers went to her mouth reflexively as her father's words washed over her.

That stupid video. Everything had started with that.

'I lied about my work because of Sabine, Dad, because of this!' Essie said, throwing her hand in the direction of the Faraday cage. 'And if Anna was helping you, how did she end up dead?'

Even as the question left her lips, she wished she could bite it back. She didn't want to know the answer. Not if it meant her father was a killer. There was still a chance it was all a horrible mistake, and he could explain everything. But her father's face fell, and he wouldn't meet her eyes.

'Oh, that was a true act of fatherly devotion,' Sabine broke in. 'When daddy dearest saw that Anna had humiliated his precious daughter in front of all those people, he simply snapped. Fortunately, I'd already fed Anna some of my blood. Contingency.'

It felt like the room tilted, throwing Essie off balance. She reached for David. His arm circled her waist, steadying her.

'It was an accident,' her father stammered. 'Anna wasn't supposed to humiliate you like that, in public! I went to her flat. We fought and she fell backwards and hit her head on the coffee table.'

Essie looked to Anna for some kind of confirmation of his story, but all her attention was focused on the console and the Faraday cage. Jono had joined her at the desk, David's blow seemingly having reset his attention. Sabine tapped her heeled boot on the stone floor impatiently, drawing Essie's gaze back to her.

'I'll admit it was a little ahead of schedule. And then Gilbert lied about what had happened to her. So poor Anna had to suffer the indignity of being dragged off to the morgue before I could retrieve her body.' Sabine threw a wry smile in Anna's direction. 'And of course, it brought us to the detective's notice as well. I had thought the Amaranthine might *finally* have died out. It had been so long. But I'm nothing if not adaptable.'

Essie barely registered anything Sabine was saying. 'You are *not* my father,' she said, shaking her finger at Gilbert. 'The man who raised me would never have done any of this. And he wouldn't have left a woman for dead.'

Her father's face crinkled at the edges and then hardened. 'The man who raised you was only half himself, Ess. You've never been in love. You don't know what it is to go through life feeling like a part of yourself is missing the entire time. But Sabine understood. She knows what it's like to lose the love of your life.'

Essie shook her head as hot anger rose inside her.

'You think I didn't miss mum, too? You think losing her justifies what you have done? What Sabine has done? The Bloodborns attacked me. I ended up in hospital. Tony would have killed me if it weren't for David.'

'I never wanted you to get hurt, Ess. If the detective

hadn't started sniffing around, none of that would have been necessary. Once I realised you had lied about solving Zion's Loop, I thought you'd have some record of your work somewhere. You are messy and slightly disorganised, but you always kept meticulous notes when it came to your work.'

The Faraday cage sparked and fizzled. Gilbert's gaze was drawn to it.

'And now we can have a second chance. So can Sabine. I can go back and save your mother. And you,' he smiled.

Shaking her head, Essie backed away from her father slowly, hot tears stinging at her eyes. Sabine appeared behind him and draped her delicate arm around his shoulder.

'Dear, sweet Gilbert, all he wants is to see his darling Rhonda again. And I do understand.' She threw a glance at David.

'But first . . .' she said, tilting her father's head to one side and plunging her teeth into the soft flesh of his neck.

'No!' Essie screamed, moving towards him automatically. David grabbed her arm, pulling her firmly back towards him. Sabine lifted her mouth from her father's neck and licked the blood from her lips.

'It's all right,' he said, holding his hand against his neck. 'She only takes enough to keep her strength.' A trickle of red ran out over his hand and a stain bloomed against the white of his shirt collar. Sabine shot a gleeful smile at Essie over her father's shoulder.

Bile stung Essie's throat, and she swallowed hard to stop herself from throwing up. For almost two years, she had prayed that her father was not dead, but now she wondered if this wasn't worse than what she had feared. He was not dead, but he was not himself. The man who stood before her was a hollow version of who he used to be.

'I can't let you do this, Dad. What Sabine told you is all lies.'

'No, your detective is the liar,' her father shot back. He spun around and pointed a shaking finger at David. 'Ask him about the night of the car accident that killed your mother. Ask him to tell you why he was there but did nothing to help. The Amaranthine, so noble and honourable, but he didn't save Rhonda or you. Instead, he protected himself, protected what he is,' Gilbert spat.

Essie's brow creased in confusion as she turned to David.

'What's he talking about? What does he mean you were there?'

David's eyes grew darker until they were almost black. Essie's heart tightened.

'It's true.' His voice was rough, shaky. 'The night of your family's car accident was the first time I met you. I had just become a police officer here. I was the first on the scene.'

Essie could almost feel the cold rain again as it fell through the destroyed roof of the vehicle, hitting her cheeks and hair. A memory broke through the surface of her consciousness. Back then, he had been a stranger at the car window, but now she could place his familiar, gentle voice.

'I remember. I remember you saying you couldn't hear my mother's heart. I was trapped in the car . . . you told me everything would be all right . . . and then . . .'

She touched the mottled skin of her hand, felt the searing burn again, heat like she'd never known before. Every nerve had been screaming with pain before her mind had mercifully plunged her into darkness.

'Why didn't you tell me?'

David shook his head. 'To tell you about the car accident when we met again would have meant telling you everything, who I really am.'

'Is it true? That you could have saved us?' He dropped his gaze.

'When I arrived at the scene, it was already too late to help your mother. As I spoke to you through the window, the car burst into flames. I wanted to get you out, but others had arrived – a fire truck, paramedics. I couldn't help you without exposing my unique abilities, my mission.'

'So, you left me there? To burn?' Her voice was barely a whisper.

'The way I failed you that night has haunted me, always,' David said, bowing his head to his chest.

Essie swung her head towards the Faraday cage. It hissed and arced with electricity. The rainbow circle was picking up speed. The air in the room reverberated through her head, like the noise in a car going at high speed with one window open. She put her hands over her ears to muffle the sound. Papers and rubbish took flight inside the cage, like gigantic, misshapen snowflakes spinning through the air, finding their way towards the wormhole.

Essie stepped back in David's direction and felt his hand on the small of her back.

'What's happening?' he mouthed.

'The density of the wormhole is generating its own magnetic field, and it's growing. Everything is being pulled towards it. Like a black hole.'

'Show time!' Sabine shouted, pulling the blond vampire towards the altar stairs. 'Time to make yourself useful, Jono!' She pushed him through a hinged door in the cage wire, like the airlock in a submarine. Jono hesitated a moment, staring at the flashing circle. Sabine closed the door and secured the latch.

'It's going to be all right, isn't it, Annie? You know what you're doing, right?'

'Yes, I know what I'm doing,' she snapped back, without looking up.

Heavier objects began hurtling towards the Faraday cage. Old hymnbooks flew open and up like doves. Essie ducked as wooden splinters from shattered rows of pews darted past her head like arrows. A plastic chair skittered up the aisle before it lifted from the ground and slammed into the cage, denting the wire and breaking the chair into fragments. The Faraday cage would not be strong enough to counter the wormhole's pull for long.

She struggled to keep her feet planted as the invisible force acted on her, drawing her in. David's arms wrapped around her, and he whisked them both behind the church's transept wall. He held onto her tightly as the stone barrier buffered some of the force, offering a level of respite from the unrelenting pull.

Essie peeked her head around the corner. Jono's dreadlocks were plastered against his face by the whirlpool's crosswinds. His boots slid across the floor as if it were oil slick, and he turned and gripped the wire frame of the cage, white knuckled, as his feet swept out from under him. He twisted his alarmed face towards Anna.

'What's happening?' he cried. Anna said nothing, and then a second later, he vanished, rocketing inside the wormhole.

Whole church pews shook and rocked on their feet. Bits of iron rivets and loose stones slowly worked their way across the stone floor. The large floodlight flickered and tottered briefly on its tripod before crashing to the floor, the bulb shattering, veiling the whole church in darkness but for the growing blue light of the wormhole.

Sabine turned her head, searching for Essie.

'What's wrong?' she screamed, staggering backwards, still clutching Gilbert by the neck. She struggled to get clear of the magnetic pull, moving like her feet were stuck in deep mud. She managed to drag herself and Gilbert behind the opposite transept wall across the aisle from David and Essie.

There was an ear piercing sound like nails running down a blackboard. Essie watched as the Faraday cage began to buckle and twist in on itself. The whole structure collapsed and crunched again and again, until it was no bigger than a paper clip. Essie glanced across the aisle and saw Sabine's waxen features transformed with mute horror.

Now that there was no longer any metal barrier buffering the vortex, everything that was not nailed down was pulled towards the hole. The toppled floodlight quickly disappeared. Anna's scream echoed through the church. She clung to the radiometer for a moment before losing her grip. In a flash of red curls and blue light, the wormhole swallowed her up. The quantum computer lifted from the ground and followed after her.

'Fix it!' Sabine choked, 'or I'll kill your father!'

Essie pressed her back into the stone wall, grateful for its steadfastness as she tried to catch her breath. David leaned towards her.

'Can you stop it, Essie?' he shouted, the crosswinds whipping strands of his hair into a matted frenzy. A long, slow shudder rippled out from the altar.

'I don't know,' she shouted back, trying to make herself heard over the din. 'I think the wormhole's density will eventually stabilise, and then the magnetic field should balance out, but the limits are untested. I don't know if that will happen before or after this entire church is sucked in and us along with it!'

David nodded, trying unsuccessfully to push the hair out of his eyes.

'Can you reverse it?'

'Not without the control panel on the computer. The only way to stop it now is to manually shut down the power to the temporal radiometer or destroy the magnet,' Essie said, pointing at the giant black rectangle near the altar. David nodded and eased himself up, using the wall for support. Essie tugged the arm of his suit jacket.

'We have to save my dad. I know he's done some terrible things, but he's my father. If there's any way, we have to try.'

'We will,' David promised, closing his hand over hers. 'But first, I need to deal with Sabine.'

Essie blinked, and he was gone from her side.

Chapter 29

David

There was only one way to kill a Bloodborn vampire. But without the sword Sabine had cast aside into the darkness, David would need to improvise. Standing on the back of a pew, he jumped, propelling himself to the church's gallery. On long ago Sunday mornings, he imagined a choir would have occupied the upper stalls where he stood, or perhaps a couple of late-comers sneaking into the service unobserved. But the elaborate stained-glass windows behind had long ago been vandalised or given way to the elements, and the colourful remnants lay strewn across the gallery carpet. David picked up a slender shard and carefully stowed it in the interior pocket of his jacket.

The high vantage point afforded him a view of the whole nave. In the swirling light of the vortex, he could see Sabine plastered against the northern transept. She held Gilbert closely. Essie crouched against the opposite transept. He couldn't see Rafael.

'The wormhole's appetite is insatiable, Sabine. Soon it will swallow us all, unless we shut it down,' David shouted down to her.

'Make the doctor fix it or I will kill her father.' David could see she was struggling to hold on to her hostage and maintain her current position in the face of the wormhole's overwhelming pull.

'She can't do anything now,' David answered. 'The computer went into the vortex with your friends. It is out of control.'

Sabine's animal cry of despair was far from her usual melodic voice. It was carried through the church by the crosswinds of the vortex. A first-row church pew finally became unhinged and flew at speed into the vortex, followed by its counterpart across the aisle. The gateway's power appeared to grow at a rate of knots. Like a hungry child, its yawping mouth was devouring everything in its path.

There was a rustle below, then a familiar figure flickered across the nave. *Rafael*. He was moving with enough momentum to avoid the magnetic field. Sabine's eyes tracked him too, but she was too occupied keeping her own position and holding onto her hostage to take any defensive action. She readjusted her grip on Gilbert's slight frame, his eyes growing wide at the destructive power unfolding before him.

David vaulted down from the gallery into the nave, landing outside the reach of the force field.

'This is finished, Sabine,' he shouted over the noise. 'Release him.'

Rafael blurred across the nave again, and when David's eyes skipped back to Sabine, Gilbert was gone. He brandished the glass shard from his jacket and launched himself at Sabine, the sharp edge slicing through the air. She dodged the blade infinitesimally, twisting out of its path and falling into the full strength of the gravitational field. Levelled to the ground by its overwhelming power, she clawed at the stone floor as the invisible force dragged her feet first towards the altar.

'No!' she howled, floundering around like a fish, trying pointlessly to slow her pace. Rafael appeared from the shadows, torpedoing Sabine's flapping body, and sending them both reeling up the aisle towards the church entrance. Flipping her on her back, he ground his knee into her chest. David caught the shimmer of a blade high above the older vampire's head. Sabine writhed under Rafael's knee, spluttering and gasping. Her violet-grey eyes flitted briefly to David as Rafael brought the sword down. Her platinum blonde head was cleaved neatly from her slender body. It rolled down the aisle, coming to rest against the base of a pew, a macabre, hollow-eyed melon.

David let out a deep sigh and slumped to his knees.

The sword clattered from Rafael's hand onto the stone floor as he collapsed back onto his haunches.

Chapter 30

Essie

The unweighted mass of Sabine's corpse skittered across the floor before sailing up the aisle and disappearing into the vortex. Essie looked about frantically for her father, her eyes finding him across the aisle where Rafael had tethered him to a pew end using his waist belt.

Essie locked eyes with him.

'Stay there, Dad,' she shouted. 'I've got to shut it off.'

He turned his face and shook his head. His hands were busy working at the belt buckle, the only thing anchoring him in place.

'Don't do that, Dad. You'll fall into the wormhole.'

'I have to, Ess,' he cried over the clamour of the vortex. The crosswinds glued his hair back from his face as if he were riding a rollercoaster. 'I have to right my wrongs.'

Essie strained forwards, trying to figure out how she could get to the wires behind the pulpit and avoid being sucked into the vortex herself. The radiometer was drawing a lot of power. She had to find the source and cut it off before her father did something crazy.

Turning back to him, she pleaded. 'There are no wrongs, Dad. The accident wasn't your fault. It was no one's fault. Just stay there.'

'But I can change the past, Ess. I can save your mother's life. We wouldn't have to live with this constant ache, the hole inside that can never be filled.' His face was lined with fear and pain. He clutched his closed fist to his heart.

Essie squeezed her eyes shut. She understood exactly what he meant. The ache, the hole inside. It opened again like a chasm as she heard the screeching of the car brakes on the slick road. The jolt of the impact, the car tumbling over. She felt the snap of her seatbelt crushing her tiny body. She heard her mother's soft moans, what must have been her final breaths. She felt the agony of the burns, the skin grafts. She thought about Cecil, and the hospital machines beeping, and how pale he had looked, how cold his hand was in hers. She thought about the pain that flooded her senses when the doctors couldn't make him breathe again, and how it had made another hole in her fragile heart. Every fibre of her body ached with loss. What wouldn't she give to not feel this way anymore.

Her hand found the tiny bicycle charm at her neck and clasped it tightly. Then a warm hand linked fingers with her, and she opened her eyes. David stood beside her, tall and steady. Rafael was behind him. David's words to her after Cecil died echoed through her mind. *The pain is part of it.* She refocused her eyes on her father's shaking form as he continued to struggle with the belt.

'It's meant to hurt, Dad. I know that sounds strange. But when a connection like you had with mum is broken, it is always going to be painful. The pain is part of the loving. It hurts so much because you loved her so much. And loving is how we know we are still alive.' Her cheeks were wet, tears streaming down them.

The roaring noise from within the vortex grew louder and Essie raised her hands to her ears, trying to block it out. Smoke streamed out from behind the altar as the temporal radiometer kicked up a gear. The acrid smell of melting plastic and burnt metal filled her nostrils. The radiometer was overheating. If they didn't shut it down soon, the whole church, and perhaps even beyond it, would be torn up in the slipstream.

She glanced across the aisle again. Her father's trembling fingers were still frantically working to undo the belt buckle. He wasn't listening.

Essie willed him to stop, to look at her. The wind whipped her hair into her eyes, blinding her. The stone floor quaked beneath them. She pushed the locks from her forehead and set her face towards her father again.

Look at me.

His hands stilled, releasing the buckle, and after a long moment, his face crinkled and fell. When he finally looked up at Essie, his cheeks were wet too.

'Oh Essie, what have I done?'

As the words left his mouth, the loosened belt flew away. He hovered momentarily before shooting forwards.

He caught the edge of the altar stair tenuously. Essie moved out from behind the wall towards him. Without the protection of the transept wall, she fell into in the full force of the magnetic field, her feet swept out from under her like being caught in the undertow of a wave. She lay plastered to the ground, watching as her father struggled, finally losing his grip.

The light of the vortex grew blindingly bright and the air around Essie exploded with a sonic boom. Her stomach lurched as her body was abruptly propelled off the ground. Tendrils of lightning issued from the radiometer, illuminating all the dark recesses of the church, and Essie was weightless, suspended in space, as the shock wave coming from the vortex propelled her away from the wormhole. Shooting up the aisle of the church, she crashed into something solid but soft. David cradled her fall as they crashed onto the stone floor together. Essie threw her arm over her face to shut out the blinding light and David pulled her into his broad chest, shielding her as the wormhole emitted another lighting strike. Another sonic shock wave thundered through her ears as she buried her face into David's shirt. His arms tightened around her, and then there was silence.

The mood in the church was eerie in the sudden stillness. The wind had dropped, and all the papers and detritus caught up in the slipstream floated to the ground, settling around them. Essie opened her eyes and sat up. The particle board covering the rose window over the altar had been blasted away by the force. Dispersed light spilled through the gaping hole, falling over the altar. Essie's eyes searched the space anxiously. The heavy wooden structure and even the torture rack were still largely intact, somehow having withstood the blast of energy. The wormhole was gone. And her father was nowhere to be seen. Her heart shattered. Collapsing back into David's embrace, she closed her eyes and wept.

Chapter 31

David

The day after the events at the church, David stood in front of Morton and his team. He gave them a falsified debrief of the last twenty-four hours, light on details. Leads he was following had come to a dead end. They would need to regroup. Something could still turn up. He knew Morton suspected something else. But she seemed to trust him enough to let it go for now.

Meanwhile, the strange disappearance of Anna Steenberger's body had taken on legendary status. The coroner's office had announced the installation of new security measures in response, but general interest in the murder case ebbed. As was often the case, the news cycle moved on to something else. A local celebrity couple were divorcing and the husband's mistress had turned up dead. Inspector Jameson ordered David's team to redirect resources into the new homicide investigation. David felt he had got lucky this time. But it was a reminder that he was living on borrowed time. It would get harder and harder to conceal the truth of his existence now. Something would have to change. Yet he was more reluctant than ever to move on.

FOUR DAYS after the events at the church, David stood at Essie's front door and knocked.

'Hi,' she said. Sweet cloves and soap swept over him in a familiar tide as he took her in. Her blonde hair was out, hanging in waves over her shoulders, her blue eyes as piercing as ever.

'Hi,' he replied. She stood back to let him into the house.

'So, there's still no sign of my father?' She asked as they sat down with cups of tea.

'No, I'm afraid not.'

'I thought the blast might have knocked him out of the way. But he must have gone into the wormhole with the rest of them,' she said. 'I'm not sure about the Bloodborns, but dad couldn't have survived it. He must be dead.'

'I'm so sorry I couldn't get to him.'

'It's not your fault. You tried to help him. We all did.'

David hadn't had to do much to cover up the scene at the church and prevent any further inquiry. The grey cloud gathering overhead as he entered the church was the herald of an extreme weather event crossing the Great Australian Bite. An unprecedented storm cell. High rainfall, lightning and thunder. The wormhole's sound and light show went completely unnoticed under the cover of mother nature's own spectacular display. The church itself had been abandoned for so long and vandalised on many occasions, which easily camouflaged any damage they had caused during the melee. And conveniently, the Bloodborns had been swallowed by the wormhole, save for Sabine's dismembered head. Rafael had taken care of that. It was now in a weighted bag at the bottom of the ocean.

But still, some things were unresolved. And David was relieved that Essie had invited him to come see her.

'I need to apologise to you,' he said. 'Your father was right. I am to blame for what happened to you when you were little.'

She had every right to hate him. He certainly hated himself. Would she ever be able to forgive him for abandoning her to her fate that night? Would she still want to have anything to do with a strange, otherworldly creature, such as himself, now that their lives were not in mortal danger?

He stole a glance at her across from him. He was anxious to gauge her thoughts, but her blue eyes were unreadable. She lifted her teacup to her mouth, took a sip, and tilted her head to the side.

'You were faced with an impossible choice, and you had a job to do. Well, two jobs. The one you signed up for over a hundred years ago, and the one you started that night.'

David frowned. 'But if I had been braver, I would have rushed into that fire and found a way to deal with the consequences.'

Her hand closed over a little charm that hung on a necklace at her throat.

'It's hard to show people who we really are. To let them in,' Essie said. 'I understand how that feels, even if I'm not trying to hide my identity as a supernatural creature on a mission to save humanity.'

'I truly am sorry, though. I-I want to ask for your forgiveness.'

'I forgave you already. And anyway, I made my own mistakes too. So many of them. It's time for both of us to have a fresh start.' She leaned across and laid her hand on his for a moment. Her touch sent a wave of warmth through his body. Her heart beat faster and colour flushed her cheeks before she sat back in her chair.

'Cecil's funeral is next week,' she said. 'Mary invited me to give the eulogy. I tried to tell her she should do it, as his family, but she insisted I was as much family to Cecil as she was.'

'I'll come with you,' he replied quickly. As soon as the words were out, he wasn't sure if he should have offered. She may have forgiven him for the past, but was that the kind of thing she wanted from him now? Or did she want to leave him and his dark, complicated world behind?

'That would be nice,' she said, as her eyebrows drew together in a frown. 'But I don't know what to say, for the eulogy.'

'You could say what's in your heart.' Her gaze drifted from him, and she fingered the necklace again.

'I'm not very good at that. I prefer facts over feelings. It's much simpler.'

'You found the right words in the church for your father. I'm sure you will know what to say. Remember who Cecil was, and how he made you feel, and the rest will come to you.'

THE FOLLOWING WEEK, David arrived at her door again in a new suit to drive them to the service. Mary greeted them both warmly as they arrived. When it was time to give the eulogy, Essie stood on the stage, her hands gripping the lectern as her heart pounded.

'I first met Cecil when he helped me change a flat bike tyre,' she began. 'But it was what he taught me about friendship that I'll always remember. To be friends, real friends, you have to risk yourself a bit. Sometimes people might hurt you, but that's ok. You have to do it anyway. Because no one should be an island. We all need connection.'

Her eyes found David's and he smiled at her reassuringly. It was a small service, and many of those gathered had shed tears, including Essie, by the time she took her seat. David handed her his handkerchief, and she grinned at him as she took it.

'You're making a habit of lending me your handkerchief,' she sniffed quietly.

'Keep it,' he whispered, leaning towards her.

ABOUT A MONTH LATER, a young man came into the police station to report he had not been able to get in touch with his younger brother for some time. His name was Cooper Bradford. He felt guilty asking Morton to take down the details of the report, not able to face the legacy of what had happened to Anna and Jono. He would never be able to give Cooper the finality that would be a comfort in the circumstances. His brother would be a missing person forever.

But later that night, as he sat with Rafael, his friend reminded him that Anna and Jono had also made their own choices. It was not all his responsibility.

David nodded. The front page of the local paper, spread across Rafael's coffee table, caught his eye. He picked it up and read aloud.

'A beautifully preserved and very rare example of a mediaeval torture device, circa seventeenth century, was gifted to the museum by a wealthy, anonymous donor.' David glanced at Rafael before continuing.

'The unique piece, which, in a bespoke innovation, has been ornamented with sharp metal spikes on the cross-planks, has taken pride of place in the collection. It will be visited by bus loads of local school children before beginning a national tour as the centrepiece to an exhibition titled "Mediaeval Murder and Mayhem."'

David raised his eyebrows at Rafael.

'What?' Rafael said, spreading his hands expansively. 'It is genuine antique. It would be shame to waste it. I have not seen that kind of rack in centuries.'

The older vampire had recovered reasonably well from

his encounter with Sabine. But the whole ordeal had been a wake-up call to them both. There were Bloodborns still out there, ancient ones that were playing a very long game.

'Sabine said she swore her oath to Enki. Do you think she meant that literally?' David asked Rafael as they sipped red wine. 'Do you think any of those stories are real? That means she would have been over a thousand years old.'

Rafael shrugged. 'Who can say? But it is a reminder, we must remain vigilant, as always.'

David nodded. 'Sabine was a formidable adversary.'

'It would not have been possible to defeat her without you and the doctor,' Raf acknowledged, tilting his head thoughtfully. David levelled his gaze at his old friend over the rim of his wineglass. 'She showed unusual courage for a human. Thank you for coming for me.'

David straightened. 'Am I hard of hearing or did you just compliment a human?'

Rafael waved his hand dismissively. 'One bird in hand does not make it hot.' David smacked his thigh with laughter.

'What?' Rafael asked, shrugging.

'You mean "One swallow does not a summer make"?'

'*Mio Dio,*' Rafael replied. 'It is an easy mistake. English is the hardest language of all you know.'

'Sorry,' David said, regaining his composure and remembering how much he owed his friend.

'I was thinking, you should bring the doctor here for dinner one night,' Rafael said.

David's eyes flicked to his face. Had he just invited a human to dinner? In his own apartment?

A FEW WEEKS LATER, when David picked Essie up and drove her to Rafael's, he couldn't decide what was stranger. The offer of Rafael to have them over in the first place or the fact that she had accepted. But he was glad she did. More and more, he found himself wanting to be with her. He watched her quietly as she nosed around Rafael's bookshelf while Rafael cooked dinner.

'He has so many first editions,' she said to David, her voice awed. She reached for the spine of one particular book, and he heard her heart skip. As she pulled the volume from the shelf, and turned it over, he noted the title. *Infinite Possibilities: A Journey Through Quantum Mechanics* by Izaachar Zion. Essie flicked it open to the title page and David leaned over her shoulder. There in faded ink was the signature of the author himself.

'Is it the book that your father gave you when you were little?' he asked gently. She raised her eyes to meet his.

'This one's in much better condition,' she smiled, 'but yes.'

Rafael served risotto. Essie seemed sceptical of Rafael's culinary skills at first, but after she had cleaned her plate, she declared it was the only risotto she had tasted that was up to the same standard as the dish at her father's restaurant. Later, as they washed up from dinner, Raf protested she had only said that to flatter his ego. But David shook his head.

'Essie's not given to flattery, Raf. She's a scientist. She likes to stick to the facts,' he smiled, tossing a tea towel at her. She caught it and picked up a soap-warmed dish from the rack, running the towel over its shiny surface.

'He's right. I always say what I mean, for better or worse,' she grinned, placing the dried plate back in the cupboard and picking up a sudsy wine glass. 'For example, this one needs another rinse.' She handed it back to David, who sighed and plunged it back into the sink full of water.

Rafael leaned on the kitchen bench, watching them. '*Dado*, you should listen to the doctor. She is very smart,' he chuckled.

Essie's brow creased. '*Dado*.' She tried it out. 'I like it.'

'It is your Australian tradition, is it not? Nicknames. A sign of affection. A mark of brotherhood.'

David's face felt warm at Rafael's compliment, and he ducked his head.

Later, as they said goodbye, Rafael gave Essie Zion's book.

'This is for you, doctor,' he said, pressing the volume into her hand.

'No, I couldn't take it,' she said, wiping at her cheeks. 'It's a signed copy. Did you actually meet him?'

Rafael frowned and cupped his chin.

'No, I don't think so. I do not even recall how the book came into my possession, or why I still have it. So, you must take it,' he said. She held it tightly to her chest as they waved goodbye.

THE NEXT WEEK, David offered to take Essie to the Institute to talk to Angela Chu about getting her job back. He also owed the provost an update on Anna's case, which he felt was best delivered in person.

'You look a lot better, Essie, and different somehow,' Angela said from behind her impressive desk. She occupied a light-filled corner office on the second floor of the Institute, overlooking the grassed quadrangle and gardens below.

Essie nodded. 'I feel a lot better.'

'I was sorry to hear about Cecil. He was so well regarded here, and I know you two were close. It's a great loss.'

Essie's hand closed over the charm at her neck reflexively. She never took it off now, and after she had explained its origin to him, he understood why.

'Cecil was the best. There'll never be anyone like him. But I'd like to keep teaching, to honour his memory, if you'll have me back.'

Angela did not immediately answer. She turned to David.

'And what has happened with the investigation into Steenberger's death? The media seems to have dropped it completely.'

David straightened in his seat and leaned forwards. 'Yes, I'm afraid there are no more leads at present. We will monitor any developments, of course. The lack of a body makes it challenging.'

'Yes. Very odd business. I hope the coroner's office is onto that.'

'They are,' David assured her.

'Well, I'm not sure if you know, but my nephew managed to get that darn video taken down. I don't know how he did it, but he did.'

Essie raised her eyebrows. 'That's great. You must be proud of Ben.'

'I'll be prouder if he can manage to finish out the semester as your research assistant and stay out of trouble.'

A smile spread across Essie's face and David heard her heart rate rise.

'Does that mean I can come back?'

Angela tilted her head. 'The Board seems to have forgotten about everything since the media died down. And goodness knows we need you. You can have all your classes back at the start of the second teaching period.'

David sensed Essie struggling to control herself as she wriggled excitedly in her seat.

'Thanks, Angela,' she said, trying to keep her voice even.

They said goodbye and as they walked back to his car through the quadrangle, he remembered the night in the rain when they had been attacked by Sabine.

'Where do you think they are now? Could they still be alive?' he asked.

'You mean Anna and Jono? I honestly don't know. Anything I say would be speculation without more research. But that has some big implications for both of us. I don't think it's a good idea to go looking into it, not yet.' He nodded in agreement. It was too risky to go poking around. Sabine was gone, but her very existence had proven that the Bloodborns were playing the long game. There was nothing to say that there weren't more like her out there. He and Rafael had been conducting regular reconnaissance trips and Rafael had even ventured on a short trip to Italy, seeking out other Amaranthine. He hadn't found anyone, but it was safer if they didn't do anything to draw attention to Essie's work.

After David dropped Essie off at home, he returned to his flat and lay down in his bed. When he woke, he could only remember brief snatches of a dream, intertwined with conscious memories, and all of it overlaid with strong emotion. He glimpsed his sisters running towards him through a green field and Rafael at the church in Rome, laying flowers on Nika's unmarked grave. He saw Essie pushing her unruly hair out of her face, her steely blue eyes staring him down behind glasses smudged with fingerprints. In the dream, and after he awoke, he had the strong sense that when she looked at him, she was seeing him, all of him. Detective Sorrow, the Amaranthine vampire, but also David Maric, the soldier who had died over a hundred years ago. She knew who he was, who he really was, and she hadn't run. Something loosened at his core, and he felt a warmth and lightness inside that he had not known in over a century.

Chapter 32

Essie

Essie stood on Mary's sparkling white veranda overlooking the Ionian Sea. The water glinted in the sunlight, like thousands of tiny dancing crystals, dotted with the colour of the sails on the little boats. She squinted into the sun and pulled her brimmed hat down her forehead a bit further. Mary joined her.

'Do you *ever* get tired of this view, Mary?' she asked, her hand sweeping across the beautiful vista. Mary shook her head and handed Essie a glass of white wine.

'Why do you think I stayed? Came for a holiday when I was twenty-two, then met Yanni, and the rest, as they say, is history.'

Essie returned her smile as she took the wine gratefully. 'I can't believe Cecil and Sarah never made it here, over all those years!'

'He was such a homebody at heart, you know that. Happiest in his garden, with Moffatt and the birds. Sarah too, when she was alive. I never held it against them.'

Essie clasped the bicycle charm and grinned at the memory of Cecil regaling her about the pardalotes. He did love home. She could think about him fondly now, without the overwhelming tide of grief.

Mary had invited her to come and stay with her in Greece after the funeral. She thought it over for a while and after Angela said she could have her job back, she realised she would have some time on her hands before the semester started. So she had taken Mary up on it. The weather was warm and the humidity had made her curly hair even more unmanageable than usual. But despite the crowds of high summer, she loved exploring the Old Town and taking in all the wonderful architecture.

Holidays had never been her thing. But that was before her life had been turned upside down. And Mary had been so insistent. She had the same warm charm and turn of phrase as Cecil, which made Essie feel instantly at ease. Plus, it was nice to be away, to have some distance from what had happened, time to think and reflect.

She found her thoughts drifting to David quite a bit. The mere fact of his existence upended everything she knew, not just about science, but life itself. She couldn't deny how fascinating he was to her, not only as a science experiment. She had never known anyone like him. And it wasn't just that he was an immortal, supernatural being. Essie's instincts were to keep him at arm's length, like everyone else. But then Cecil's words would come back to her about not being an island.

When she told him of her travel plans, he was cautiously supportive.

'But what if something happens to you . . . we don't know if the Bloodborns . . .'

Essie shrugged. 'Something could happen to me here. It just did. I can't live my whole life in fear.'

He sighed lightly in response, a gesture Essie now recognised as his reluctant acquiescence to her.

The day before she left for Greece, she opened her front door to find him standing there, formal as ever, in a three-piece suit. He straightened his tie and smoothed his hair over.

'I . . . I was wondering, Essie,' he began haltingly, 'when you come back from Greece, would you like to go out to dinner with me sometime?'

'Is Rafael making risotto again?' she joked.

'No, I mean out to dinner, at a restaurant. Just you and me,' he said, touching his tie again.

Essie stilled herself, suppressing the urge to grin. It was not as if she herself were any authority on dating, if that was what he was attempting.

'Sounds great,' she said. 'I know this pretty good Italian place on the main street. Maybe we could go there?'

David smiled and inclined his head. 'Really? You're a frequenter of Italian restaurants? Fancy that.'

'I have one condition though,' she said, angling her head. 'You promised me you'd answer all my questions about – well – you. I have a list, remember?'

He rocked back on his heels and slipped his hand in his pockets.

'That's not really a conversation for a public place, but a promise is a promise.'

ONE SLIGHTLY COOLER EVENING TOWARDS the end of her stay in Greece, she put on a cardigan and wandered down from Mary's house to the local jetty to watch the sun set over the horizon. As she passed by a local café, in the window, she watched a man plying pizza dough. With each fluid motion, his fingers delicately pressed and pulled, coaxing it to stretch and yield. The dough responded under his skilled touch, its elasticity allowing it to effortlessly expand into a larger and more malleable shape. It reminded her of all the times she had stood watching her father perform the same practiced action. While he had been missing, she feared the worst, that he was dead. But now she knew she had not even understood what the worst could be. Losing a loved one was hard, but being betrayed by someone you love meant you lost them in a different way, a way that made it somehow impossible to say goodbye. Her brain understood her father had good intentions and that he thought he was doing the right thing, but her heart couldn't match his actions to the man who had taught her how to tie her shoelaces. At times, the dissonance between the two stole her breath. Had he been suffocating under that blanket of grief the entire time? Or were some of her happy memories happy for him as well? In as much as her mother's death had been a defining event in her life, her father had defined everything that came after that. But it turned out what she thought was a cement foundation undergirding her was actually a pillar made of sand. Her sense of self and the world around her seemed to shift under the weight of this realisation.

As Essie climbed the stairs to her house, her shoulders relaxed, and she let out a long breath. It was nice to be home again. She dropped her suitcase and put her shoulder into opening the sticky front door, only to stumble forwards into the entry when it gave way. Inside, the house looked neater and cleaner than when she had left. This and the repaired front door did not surprise her a bit. David had offered to feed Moffatt while she was away and so he had been visiting daily. He'd even sent her a few pictures of Moffatt lying in the sun or curled up in a chair. Hauling her suitcase into the entryway, she closed the door behind her and made her way to the lounge. Although she was dying for a cup of tea, she slumped down on the cushions in exhaustion. One second later, a gentle knock sounded on the front door.

She had to admit it did not displease her to find David standing there. Seeing him again after such a long time, she was jolted back to the realisation of just how otherworldly he was. She watched as his eyes changed colour from cerulean, to grey to azure, while he stood on her doorstep. A living, preternatural science experiment, wrapped in the body of a handsome man.

'You're back.' He slipped his hands into his pockets.

'Good timing, I just walked in,' she said, beckoning him

into the entryway. 'The door is fixed. That was you, I assume?'

He nodded. 'Least I could do after nearly unhinging it.'

Essie smiled. 'Do you want a cup of tea? I was just going to put the kettle on.'

'Allow me,' he replied, disappearing into the kitchen, and returning in a few moments with her old tray, carrying the tea things. Essie settled back into the armchair, yawning. Clearly, the jetlag was catching up to her. David poured the tea from the pot into the two teacups and saucers and handed one cup to Essie.

She lifted it to her lips, blowing to cool it down.

'How was Greece?' he asked.

'Just beautiful, David. And Mary was the best host. I am so glad I went.' A grey and white cat pounced onto David's lap, and he lifted his teacup over his head to prevent it from spilling.

'Moffatt,' Essie exclaimed. 'Where are your manners?' She leaned over trying to shoo him away. The cat leapt from David's knee onto the coffee table, upsetting the tray and toppling the teapot onto the carpet.

'Oh dear,' Essie said, getting down on her knees to pick it up. David, forever faster, was already there. They bumped heads and she laughed, sitting back on her haunches as she rubbed at her temple.

'I'm so sorry,' he said, his face anxious. 'Are you all right?'

'Fine,' she said. He reached out and his hand ghosted across her cheek, and tucked a stray piece of her hair behind her ear. Essie felt the heat rush to her cheeks. Even she could hear her heart, pounding out its traitorous rhythm.

She cleared her throat, and David moved back.

A terse rap on the front door caused Essie to jump.

'Are you expecting someone?'

'No,' she replied, 'but I wasn't expecting you either.'

Moffatt shadowed Essie's leg as she went to answer the door. When she opened it, she frowned as she stared at the young woman standing on her doorstep. Her dark, thick hair hung to just below her shoulders and her neck was adorned with strings of beads and a large, wire-wrapped precious stone that might have been pink quartz. She had round eyes, murky green with brown tinges on the edge. Her eyes were so familiar. Her eyes and her hair. Essie glanced from the woman to the framed family photo on her hallstand and back again. Her sudden, sharp intake of breath bought David to her side in a flash.

'Esther,' the woman said, reaching out a hand to touch her cheek. 'Look at you! All grown up.'

'Mum?' Essie whispered.

Read on for a sneak peek at the next book in this series.

Chapter 1

David

David studied his reflection in Essie's entryway mirror, straightening his tie as he held his phone to his ear with his shoulder. The day was not playing out as he imagined it. He had stopped by Essie's house to arrange the dinner date they had talked about before she left on holiday. He had almost talked himself out of the idea on the way over. He still wasn't convinced it was sensible for him to be part of her life. His world was risky and unpredictable. He didn't want to put her in danger. But he missed her while she was away. He missed her sharp eyes staring at him from behind her perpetually smudged glasses. He missed her knowing smile. And it was just dinner after all, wasn't it? But now, instead of making dinner plans, they were planning a journey to the past with Essie's long-dead mother to retrieve her father and hunt some Bloodborns.

Although it wasn't what he had anticipated, he didn't

mind the interruption. It meant he could put off answering the question of what his relationship with her was or should be for a little longer. And he had to go with her. There was no question. The Bloodborns had ended up in the past with Essie's father. They were a vampire problem which made it his problem.

The phone kept ringing. David sighed. No surprise. Raf was always mislaying his phone. He didn't care much for such modern conveniences. Essie's mother, Rhonda, said that Raf should go with them to the past. He had to admit that it would be reassuring if Raf was there. Despite his health problems, he was older and more experienced. And there was nothing he took more seriously than his vow to defeat the Bloodborns. Also, he would be furious with David, his younger sire, if he went after the Bloodborns alone. Still, he shifted his weight uneasily when Raf finally picked up the call.

He quickly updated him on the situation, then there was a long pause.

'I don't trust this Rhonda woman, *Dado*. How we know this is not trap of Bloodborns?' He spoke in broken English, accented by his Italian heritage.

David sighed. 'We don't I suppose. But what choice do we have?'

Raf grunted down the end of the line. David could almost hear the older man thinking and waited for what would come next.

'So, what about the dream you have?'

The dream. A shiver iced up David's neck, and he tried

to shake it off. In the past, his dreams had been a welcome experience. It was one reason he still slept, even though as an Amaranthine he didn't need sleep anymore. Memories came to him in dreams, vignettes from his long ago past.

After Raf had turned him, he went back home to see his family for the last time. Raf warned him against it. Better they think him dead since he could never tell them the truth. But he had gone anyway, lingering near the small village where he grew up. He stayed in the shadows as he followed them on the walk back to the Maric family home. Watching from outside the modest cabin, his heart ached as he saw them together, breaking bread for their evening supper. His mother's long, heavy plait hung over her shoulder when she leaned to serve the food. His sisters placed their napkins delicately in their laps.

But realising Raf was right, that there was nothing he could say to them that would make them understand, he took one last glance before he turned away and never went back.

And they were all gone now. Buried in a lonely cemetery near the village church. David didn't even have any pictures of them. The Marics had no money for photographs or sketches. Even if they did, his father would have frowned upon such wastefulness and vanity. Now his dreams were where he saw his mother and sisters, sometimes even his father. He had always welcomed those fleeting night-time glimpses of his life before, even if for just a moment.

Then early one morning, while Essie was away in Greece, he had awoken with a start, pulling in gasps of air, as if all the oxygen had been sucked out of his bedroom. His heart raced and sweat beaded across his forehead. The images that had filtered up in his unconscious defied description. Amaranthine vampires – many hereditary pairs like him and Rafael – tortured, gutted, and beheaded. Their bodies lay discarded, mounded in a broken pile, and a dark, hooded figure stood over them. Blood ran unceasingly from the corpses, pooling on the floor. A horrific tableau. But it was the dream's end that haunted him the most. The first time he had the dream he thought it was an aberration. Now, every time he tried to sleep, the visions assailed him, completely overtaking the pleasant memories and darkening his sleep.

'Perhaps it is warning,' Raf had said, when David finally shared the dream with him, although he had not been able to talk about the dream's ending. But a warning about what? The Amaranthine had to be scarce in numbers now. He and Raf had not come across another like them for over a century. At first Raf said it wasn't that unusual. Time had a different meaning for them. The passage of decades could feel momentary. And the Amaranthine lived largely solitary existences, save for if they had a hereditary mate. It was safer that way. It attracted less attention from the humans. But lately, even Raf had begun to speculate if the two of them might be the last.

Yet there were a multitude of Amaranthine bodies in the dream. Pair upon pair. And the hooded figure stood triumphantly over them all. David never saw the figure's face, but somehow, he felt the figure was smiling, gleeful.

He shook himself, shifting the phone to his other ear. 'It's just a dream, Raf. I don't think it means anything.'

Raf tutted on the end of the line. 'All right. Answer another question. Do you go to past to deal with Bloodborns, or because Essie asks?'

David laughed. 'She didn't ask, Raf. She actually told me not to come. I insisted I should go. It could be dangerous. She needs protection.'

The older vampire sighed. 'She is mortal, *Dado*. You cannot protect her forever.'

He didn't know how to respond to that. He didn't know what to tell himself, let alone what to say that would convince his friend. The only word he could use to describe his feelings for Essie was conflicted. But even that didn't seem adequate. And he had no idea how she felt about him. At length, Raf exhaled, relenting.

'Where we meet?'

He smiled to himself. 'I'm at Essie's house. Meet us here.'

Raf grunted. 'I bring supplies. We feed before we leave.'

As he ended the call, David realised he didn't even know what 'leaving' would mean. What were the mechanics of time travel? How would they be transported to the past?

A scent washed over him. The high note was lavender, but there were hints of sweet cloves as well, like Essie. He turned to find Rhonda standing in the entryway with him. In the flesh, he could see that mother and daughter were similar and yet different. Essie's blue eyes had come from Gilbert, since Rhonda's were a pale green. Her dark hair contrasted Essie's lighter colour. But the corners of their mouths turned up in the same way, and they both tilted their heads to the side when they were concentrating.

'You'll need to leave that here.' She pointed at his mobile phone. 'We don't have those where I come from. The future Essie warned me not to dabble with technology. She also told me to make sure we don't bring anything back with us. She specifically said you and Rafael shouldn't try to bring any weapons. They can't pass through the wormhole. I was meant to tell you that.'

He nodded as he placed the phone carefully on the entry table and emptied his pockets of his keys and notepad. 'I don't have any weapons on me right now anyway, and I'll be sure to tell Raf.'

They went back into the lounge room as Essie was coming down the stairs. She had showered and changed into a fresh set of clothes. Her hair was wound in a wet knot at the back of her head and her glasses were slightly askew. He watched her descend the rest of the stairs. A warm, almost electric feeling surged through him. He knew he was staring but he couldn't drag his gaze away. Shaking himself, he adjusted his collar.

Rhonda's face lit up as Essie reached the bottom of the stairs. 'Look at you, Essie, so grown up. I can still hardly believe my eyes.'

Essie smiled at her mother tentatively. Her reaction to Rhonda's arrival had been, justifiably, cautious. It wasn't every day your dead mother turned up on your doorstep. And her uncertainty was still palpable in the look she gave Rhonda.

'Mum, I have a few concerns with your plan. The last time I opened a wormhole, I nearly destroyed a church and sucked half the city in with it. How do I know that won't happen again? And how do we control the destination?'

Rhonda held out her wrist to them, showing a white, matte-finish bracelet that resembled a fitness tracker.

'You solved all those problems, Ess. Well, the future you will solve them. We can travel using this.' She reached out to touch the bracelet. It lit up. Her eyebrows knit together in concentration.

'You called it the Time Weaver.'

Essie arched an eyebrow at her mother. 'That doesn't sound like a name I would use. It's so . . . abstract.' She held her mother's wrist carefully, inspecting the bracelet. 'But how did I miniaturise the technology? And stabilise the gravitational force?'

David peered over Essie's shoulder to see the Time Weaver. He didn't understand the science the way she did, of course, but in the church when they had fought Sabine, there were giant magnets that formed part of a temporal radiometer which was powering the wormhole. The setup was huge and had drawn on an enormous amount of energy. It seemed impossible all of that could be contained in a tiny wrist band, no bigger than a watch.

'I don't know how exactly,' Rhonda said apologetically. 'You tried to explain it to me, but . . . it's complicated. The important thing is you do figure it out. You also work out how to control the travel destination – mostly.'

Essie shook her head slowly. 'When do I do this? And why didn't the future me just go and get Dad from your time instead? Or why not come here to see me herself? Why did she send *you* to get me?'

Rhonda looked thoughtful as she lightly touched the bracelet, causing the light to power off. 'You were worried your dad would freak out if the future version of you came to get him and that he wouldn't listen to her.'

Essie chuckled lightly. 'How far in the future did I come from to see you? Did I look so old and wrinkled Dad wouldn't recognise me?' She brushed some stray hair out of her face self-consciously.

'There are rules,' Rhonda said. 'I'll explain that in a minute. But this version of you, now, is the one your father saw most recently, in the church. It will make it easier for him to accept that he needs to return here, to his present.'

David tried to picture Essie in ten or twenty years, her hair slowly fading to grey, her face softened and lined with age. Would she take more after Gilbert or Rhonda as the years passed by? The vision of an older Essie spurred a long-suppressed ache inside him. Growing old was something he would never get to experience, let alone growing old with someone else. It was one of the many human things he had been forced to give up. He pushed the thought away and cleared his throat.

'Rhonda, did the future Essie say anything about how we find Gilbert and the Bloodborns in the past?'

Rhonda turned her attention to him, nodding. 'I'm supposed to explain that when we get there. But before we leave, we need to go over the ground rules. There are three rules for time travel. They must be obeyed, no matter what.' She locked eyes with Essie. 'You made me memorise them.'

'Okay. What are the rules?'

Rhonda held up her index finger.

'First rule: You cannot time travel to the same place twice. You explained that time is like a delicate web. If you put too much pressure on the same thread, the web is weakened and will eventually snap. So this must be a one-off visit.'

Essie nodded. 'Okay.'

'Second rule: You can't interact with your past selves. Again, time is a delicate web. That kind of thing could snap the thread.'

'Well, that probably explains why the future Essie didn't come to see me.'

Rhonda nodded. 'And third rule: You must not change past events. No matter how tempted you are. This could destroy the web of time completely.'

David rubbed his chin as he contemplated the instructions. The analogy of time as a web was discomforting, both in its implied fragility and in how much it made it sound like they were heading into a trap.

Essie crossed her arms over her chest sullenly. 'But what does that mean – don't change past events? How do we stop events from changing? Just by going to the past we could change things.'

Rhonda's shoulders lifted in a slight shrug. 'The future Essie said that you would understand what it meant when you got there.'

Essie huffed. 'You know, Mum, future Essie seems quite cryptic.'

He had to agree with that. So far, they had little concrete information and the whole plan seemed unnecessarily convoluted. Moffatt appeared at Essie's feet and rubbed his long body against her leg as he purred. Essie's adopted cat had taken to him a little while she was away, even letting him pat him on one or two occasions when he had come over to feed and check on him. Essie reached down to scratch behind his ear.

'What about Moffatt? I'll need to get another cat sitter. And what about my job? The new semester starts in a few days. And there's a ball I'm supposed to attend. The Institute's going to announce a scholarship in honour of my friend, Cecil. He . . . he died recently.' She clasped the chain around her neck. It held a gold bicycle charm. She always wore it – a final gift from Cecil.

Rhonda patted the band on her wrist. 'You don't need to worry about any of that. Although the location can still be off a bit, no matter how long we are gone, you can return at the exact moment we leave. No time will have passed here at all. Moffatt won't even know you were gone, and you'll be back to start the semester.'

Essie looked to him again, her face ambivalent. He smiled, trying to hide his own concern. He was convinced it was the right thing for them to go. They also had little other choice. Yet there were many unknowns. For a start, where were they going? What if they weren't successful in bringing Gilbert back? What if they couldn't find the Bloodborns or they were already wreaking havoc in the past? What if something went wrong and they were stuck there indefinitely?

A sharp knock dragged their collective attention to the front door. Essie stepped past her mother to open it.

Raf stood there waiting, his face edged with a serious expression and a duffle bag slung over his shoulder.

'Hi, Rafael. Thanks for coming. Let me introduce you to my mother.'

to continue Essie and David's story, read In Time's Shadow

Acknowledgments

Writing can be a solitary pursuit. A lot of it happens when I'm alone – I first met Essie and David when they started talking to each other in my head. But getting a book published, bringing that story to the page, is definitely a team sport. I am so grateful to each person who has surrounded me on this journey. The risk of trying to name them is I will inevitably forget someone. But here goes anyway. To my mum, who has always supported all my dreams, and is a published writer herself – thank you. To my friends who read various drafts of this book: Kate Midena, Lara Wood-Gladwin, Briah McKinnon-Collins and Veronica Poland – you are amazing! And to Layla Baker-Gabb, one of my first readers, who loved what she read and was kind enough to give me honest feedback – thank you! I wouldn't have gone on without the encouragement from you all.

To my friends who contributed specialised knowledge on particular scenes. Some of you aren't named but know who you are. To my sister-in-law, Andrea Willson, an emergency department nurse with years of experience under her belt, thank you for your expertise on life and death situations and critical patient care. Any mistakes are my own.

To my amazing editor, Lacey Braziel. I connected with you all the way across the world via Instagram, and you were just exactly who I needed! Thank you for guiding me through the developmental stage, and your encouragement and skill in polishing this book from the rough diamond to what it is now. And to Cassie Weaver – thank you for your design and formatting expertise.

Finally, to my husband and my girls. You have put up with me spending hours and hours at the computer drafting, re-drafting, editing and planning. You have tip-toed past to give me peace and quiet and bought me cups of tea and biscuits to keep me sustained. You have read drafts, cheered me on and supported me from the sidelines every step of the way. I couldn't have done it without you.

Lastly, just like the story of Bezalel building the tabernacle, any creativity or skill I have in writing stories is because of the free gift of God in my life: 'I have filled Bezalel with the Spirit of God, with wisdom, with understanding, with knowledge and with all kinds of skills,' Exodus 31:3.

About the Author

TP Donohue is an Australian writer who blends fantasy, science fiction and the supernatural. An avid reader, she grew up dreaming of one day sharing her own stories with the world. She is drawn to good coffee, autumn leaves, and an early night. Her short stories have been published in fiction anthologies, and the Amaranthine Vampires Trilogy is her first book series.

Find out more about her books and sign up to be first to receive updates at www.tpdonohuewriter.com.